Elizabeth glanced up with alarm as a loud rumble broke the silence of the cave. Her eyes widened as she saw debris loosening from the walls. With a crack one of the support beams split and swung down, nearly hitting her in the back of the head. The mine shaft was collapsing!

I have to get out of here now! Elizabeth screamed silently. She spun around frantically, trying to determine which path led to the mouth of the cave. She grabbed the bag of glittering treasure and ran, praying that she'd be able to find her way out before the earth caved in around her.

She covered her head with her hands and stumbled on, feeling her eyes burn with a mix of sweat, dust, and tears. Blood pounded in her head as Elizabeth fought to quell her rising hysteria. . . . Was she about to die?

THE TREASURE OF
DEATH VALLEY

Written by
Kate William

Created by
FRANCINE PASCAL

BANTAM BOOKS
NEW YORK · TORONTO · LONDON · SYDNEY · AUCKLAND

RL 6, age 12 and up

THE TREASURE OF DEATH VALLEY
A Bantam Book / May 1995

Sweet Valley High® is a registered trademark of Francine Pascal
Conceived by Francine Pascal
Produced by Daniel Weiss Associates, Inc.
33 West 17th Street
New York, NY 10011
Cover art by Bruce Emmett

ISBN: 0-553-56633-4

Published simultaneously in the United States and Canada

Bantam Books are published by Bantam Books, a division of Bantam
Doubleday Dell Publishing Group, Inc. Its trademark, consisting of the
words "Bantam Books" and the portrayal of a rooster, is Registered in
U.S. Patent and Trademark Office and in other countries. Marca
Registrada. Bantam Books, 1540 Broadway, New York, New York 10036.

PRINTED IN THE UNITED STATES OF AMERICA

OPM   0 9 8 7 6 5 4 3 2 1

To Ada Szeto and Michael Rubin

Chapter 1

"Wake up, Todd—I think we're almost there!" exclaimed sixteen-year-old Elizabeth Wakefield. Through the van's mud-splattered windshield she spotted some buildings up ahead.

"Hrmphh," replied Todd Wilkins, Elizabeth's boyfriend. He pulled his head up from its resting place on Elizabeth's shoulder, pushing a lock of brown hair back from his face. He rubbed his eyes and looked out the window. They passed the buildings but didn't slow down. "Guess that's not the drop-off," Todd said sleepily.

"Have you ever seen so much open space?" Elizabeth continued. "Isn't this amazing? This trip is going to be so cool."

"Gee, Liz. Four days walking across sand, rock, and dirt, frying like bacon in the hot sun. You sure know how to have a good time!" Todd joked, awake now.

1

"Oh, Todd. You know it's not going to be like that. In its own way, Death Valley is incredibly beautiful. And it's lined by mountains."

"Do you think you two could keep it down up there? I'm trying to get some sleep," came the groggy voice of Jessica Wakefield, Elizabeth's twin sister.

Jessica, Elizabeth, Todd, and three other students from Sweet Valley High—Jessica's boyfriend, Ken Matthews; Heather Mallone; and Bruce Patman—were all on their way to the drop-off point for a four-day camping trek in Death Valley.

Elizabeth had been ecstatic when she'd found out that the Sweet Valley Survival School (SVSS) was conducting a required, schoolwide essay contest to pick six kids for a survival trek designed especially for high-school leaders. The assignment had been to explain how she could benefit from a course that tested her intellect, resourcefulness, and ability to work with others—right up her alley. The minute she started writing, Elizabeth had known she'd be chosen.

"Don't sound so cheerful, Wakefield. Why do you think they call it 'Death Valley'?" Bruce Patman leaned forward, putting his hand on the back of Elizabeth's seat. "Because people *die* out here." He snickered and slouched back into his seat, pulling his baseball cap low on his forehead.

Elizabeth and Todd looked at each other and rolled their eyes. Elizabeth knew they were thinking the same thing. *Why would anyone choose Bruce Patman for this trip?* He didn't know the

2

meaning of the word "cooperation." Bruce's father was the richest man in Sweet Valley, and Bruce thought that gave him the right to be the most obnoxious guy in town.

"I just wish everybody else was as excited as me," Elizabeth whispered to Todd. When Elizabeth had first heard about the trip, she had gone to the library and read up on survival adventures. She had been surprised to learn that many corporations sent their top executives on adventures similar to the one SVSS had planned. The philosophy seemed to be that if people could learn how to rely on each other when their lives really depended on it, they would work better together in the office. Conquering fear and taking risks were a big part of the experience, and Elizabeth couldn't wait to rise to the challenge.

"I'm sure we'll all get into it once we're out there, Liz," Todd assured her. "I mean, how psyched could we be? We've been up since three this morning." It was a six-hour drive between the small southern-California coastal town of Sweet Valley and the spot where they'd begin their hike into Death Valley. "And after last weekend . . ."

"You're right," said Elizabeth, opening the window to let in some fresh air. "I guess the weekend was pretty intense."

In preparation for the trip, the group had spent their Saturday and Sunday on the campus of SVSS, learning to read maps and compasses, as well as practicing other basic camping, mountaineering, and survival skills. They'd also gotten long lectures on the importance of working as a team.

3

"How're you guys doing back there?" Kay Jansen called from the driver's seat. She and Brad Mainzer, who sat next to her in the front passenger seat, were their instructors from SVSS.

"We're fine, Kay," Elizabeth answered. "Just a little cranky." *After a whole weekend with this group, I'm surprised they haven't quit their jobs,* Elizabeth thought. Suddenly the van swerved to avoid a bumper lying in the road.

"Do you think you could watch it up there?" Jessica asked huffily, blowing her blond bangs out of her eyes.

"Sorry, kids," Kay called back.

Shifting her weight to try to keep her leg from falling asleep again, Elizabeth leaned into Todd. "Have you noticed that Jess seems a tad more, ummmm, disagreeable than usual?" she whispered into his ear.

"Nah, just her usual bratty self," Todd replied. He and Jessica didn't have a lot of love for each other, a fact that neither let Elizabeth forget.

Todd wasn't the only one who noticed the differences between the twins. Although they looked identical—from their silky blond hair and eyes the color of the Pacific Ocean, to their slim, athletic figures—their ideas about how to have a good time varied dramatically.

Elizabeth thrived on intellectual challenge—her passion was writing, and she aspired to become a novelist someday. She was already pursuing that goal by working on the school newspaper, *The Oracle*. Jessica lived for the moment. She cared

4

more about fun today than consequences tomorrow.

And while Elizabeth tended to finish all of her homework right after dinner, Jessica could often be found scribbling her assignments before the sound of the first bell at school. Jessica hated to waste precious free time on schoolwork when she could be shopping or chatting on the phone with her friends.

Jessica did have one passion—one that Elizabeth didn't understand: cheerleading. Elizabeth thought her sister should use her athletic ability to be on a team, instead of just cheering on the sidelines. But even she had to admit that Jessica was one of the most energetic and spirited cheerleaders she'd ever seen.

"Let's not talk about Jessica," said Todd huskily, taking Elizabeth's hand. "Let's talk about the fact that for four days there'll be no parents and no teachers. I can't wait for us to be all alone under the stars."

"Mmmmm," murmured Elizabeth. "Sounds wonderful. The desert can be very romantic."

"What are you two lovebirds whispering about?" Heather asked cattily.

"Yeah, what's the big powwow? Planning to ditch us so you can be alone and converge with nature?" teased Bruce.

"What if we are?" Todd said, putting a protective arm around Elizabeth.

"Wouldn't bother me," Bruce said. "Personally, I wish I could ditch all of you. It's bad enough that I had to spend all weekend with a bunch of high-school kids and miss going to Las Vegas with my dad."

"Tell me about it," Heather said with a sigh, taking a compact out of her purse. "The only way I'd ever choose to go camping is if there was a fully stocked RV, with plenty of clean sheets and towels."

"And I'm missing the biannual inventory sale at Lisette's!" Jessica lamented. Lisette's was Jessica's favorite store at the Valley Mall. "The only consolation is that we're going to miss four days of school."

"I can't believe you guys are complaining," Elizabeth said. "This isn't just a camping trip. There are people who pay a lot of money to do what we're doing for free. I feel totally privileged to have been chosen for this trip."

Elizabeth was frustrated to notice that even Todd was rolling his eyes at her. They just didn't seem to understand that this trip was going to be one of the most exciting experiences of their lives. *Maybe I'm the only one of the bunch cut out for this course,* she thought. *I hope everyone else's lack of interest doesn't prove to be a problem.*

"If Elizabeth makes one more comment about how honored she feels to have been chosen for this trip, I swear I'm going to stuff a sock in her mouth," Jessica whispered to Ken.

"Calm down, Jess," he said, stroking her forearm. "I admit Liz's perkiness may be a bit over-the-top, but she has a point. I do feel pretty lucky that my essay was picked, and after spending the weekend learning all that stuff about self-reliance, I'm starting to look forward to the adventure."

"You were complaining just as much as I was on Friday night!" Jessica said, astounded that the coolest guy in the world—Ken was the captain of the Gladiators, the Sweet Valley High football team, after all—could be excited about such a nerdy activity.

"That's because I was disappointed that we couldn't spend the weekend by ourselves, like we'd planned. I've missed you," he said, taking her hand and looking deeply into her eyes.

"I've missed you, too," Jessica responded breathlessly, wishing that they were alone in the backseat of Ken's car. This hot van wasn't ideally suited for a proper kiss. Looking at her gorgeous blond boyfriend, Jessica felt overwhelmed with gratitude that their relationship had survived their recent troubles.

Months back, before Jessica and Ken had become a couple, Elizabeth had had a brief fling with Ken while Todd had been living in Vermont. For a long time neither Ken nor Elizabeth had told anyone about their fling.

But when Jessica had started seeing Ken, Elizabeth had got jealous and started to question her real feelings toward both Todd and Ken. After a lot of misunderstanding, the situation had finally been resolved. But the experience had made Jessica realize how fragile relationships could be, and the importance of honesty and communication.

Jessica leaned her head on Ken's shoulder and closed her eyes, enjoying the firmness of his muscles. After a few moments her nose twitched with an itch. When it didn't go away, Jessica touched her nose, plucking a hair off her face.

"Ouch!" squealed Heather, grabbing the back of her head. "Watch it back there."

"Well, if you wouldn't flip your hair in our faces, we wouldn't have to pull it out of your head," Jessica said with a scowl. Heather tucked her wavy mane around the side of her neck with a dramatic flair.

Jessica leaned into Ken's neck. "I'm sure I'd be a whole lot less miserable if Heather Mallone weren't on this trip. Not only do I have to spend four days in the wilderness with my least favorite person at Sweet Valley High, I'm actually supposed to get along with her!" she whispered loudly.

"I'm sure it'll be fine," Ken responded, kissing her affectionately on the cheek.

Jessica smiled and looked out the window. She tried to forget about Heather and focus instead on the dramatic cliffs that lined the highway. Then she realized that her foot had fallen asleep again. She tried to cross her legs but managed only to kick the seat in front of her.

"Do you *mind*?" Bruce snarled, turning around to glare at her.

"Sorry," Jessica said. *These darn boots are so annoyingly bulky,* she thought, wriggling in her seat to try to get comfortable. For the trip they all had to wear the geeky SVSS T-shirts, khaki shorts, and regulation hiking boots. Jessica almost refused to wear the boots when she saw how fat they made her legs look, but Elizabeth had forced her out the door before she could change.

Somehow Heather didn't look as dorky as the rest of them, Jessica realized with dismay. Sitting behind Heather, Jessica took stock of her classmate's cascade of wavy, golden tresses. Then she peeked under the seat and saw Heather's shoes. She was wearing her custom-made cheerleading shoes! Jessica sighed. She could look a lot hipper herself, if she didn't have a squeaky-clean sister who refused to realize that some rules were just too stupid to follow.

"Heather, what happened to your hiking boots?" Jessica asked sweetly. Heather swiveled her head and gazed at Jessica through lidded eyes.

"Oh, please, I wouldn't be caught dead in those ugly things," she said.

"You mean you aren't wearing hiking boots, Heather?" Elizabeth said in a surprised voice.

"No, I'm not, Liz," answered Heather. "Do you want to give me two demerits? I'm shaking in my shoes!" She laughed.

"It's for your own good that they recommended wearing hiking boots," Elizabeth said solemnly. "We're going to be traveling some tough terrain, and your feet and ankles need sturdy protection."

"These cheerleading shoes helped me survive all the way to nationals," Heather said, throwing Jessica a haughty look. "Why shouldn't they help me survive some stupid hike through the desert?"

Jessica glowered darkly. She hated to be reminded of the way the sophisticated, sexy Heather

9

Mallone had shimmied her way into the Sweet Valley High social scene and turned Jessica's world upside down. First, she'd infiltrated Jessica's cheerleading squad and ingratiated herself with all the other girls, practically forcing her way into being cocaptain. Then she'd turned all the other cheerleaders against Jessica, scheming and plotting to humiliate her until she'd finally quit the squad.

When Jessica had formed her own squad to challenge Heather's in the statewide competition, the officials had forced them to combine the two squads into one, and Jessica had been right back where she'd started: fighting Heather for everyone's respect and loyalty. When they'd made it to nationals, what should have been Jessica's shining moment had been sullied by having to share it with Heather.

"How can anyone expect me to get along with that conniving girl for four days straight?" she whispered to Ken.

"Not only will you have to get along with her," Ken said, "the way this trip is set up, you're going to have to work with her and trust her."

"Unbelievable! After all the rotten, dirty tricks she's pulled, how can they expect me to trust her?" she hissed, crossing her arms. Looking at Heather's profile, Jessica's fingers tingled with the urge to punch her cute little nose.

"You can do anything you put your mind to, Jess—even cooperate," Ken said earnestly, caressing her cheek with the back of his hand.

Jessica took his hand and held it tight. "Ken,

10

I'm the first to say that cooperation is not high on my list of best qualities," she said with a wry grin.

"Sure you're good at it, Jess. As long as everyone does everything your way, you're happy to cooperate," Ken teased.

Jessica finally cracked a smile. *Maybe it's because my way is always the right way,* she assured herself.

Elizabeth sat back in her seat and gazed out the window. The crystal-blue sky contrasted vividly against the red cliffs and hills, each color offsetting the other. A few hundred yards off the highway, a huge gray building marred the otherwise beautiful landscape.

"What's that monstrosity over there on the right?" she asked.

"The state penitentiary," Brad replied. Elizabeth shuddered—prisons gave her the creeps.

Moments later the van turned off the highway at a gas station.

"Everybody out!" Kay announced as the van rolled to a stop on the dirt-covered parking lot next to the station. "Let's all regroup over at those picnic tables," she said, hopping out.

As they settled into one of the lopsided picnic tables, Todd asked Elizabeth if she had seen the sign on the side of the road.

"What sign?"

"Right before the station there was a sign that said No Road Service for the Next Seventy-two Miles."

11

"Wow. Sounds ominous," Ken said, who was just sitting down.

"Doesn't it?" Todd concurred.

Jessica plopped down next to Ken. "Thank God. I thought I was going to get sick bouncing around back there." She had a queasy look on her face.

"Believe me—in a couple of days you'll all wish you were enjoying the comfort of bouncing around in a van," Kay interjected. She was pulling maps from her bag, laying them out on the table.

"Not very likely," Jessica said, stretching her arms over her head.

"You can stop trying to scare us now, Kay," Bruce said disdainfully. "Because I think you should know—it's not working."

"Maybe you should realize that you don't know everything, Bruce," Elizabeth said. "Kay knows what she's talking about." She looked at their instructor admiringly. Elizabeth had really come to respect Kay during their weekend of precourse training. Not only was she knowledgeable and warm, she was physically the strongest woman Elizabeth had ever met. Elizabeth wanted to grow into exactly the kind of woman Kay was.

"The time has come for you to prove your power," Kay said, looking straight at Elizabeth. Elizabeth returned her gaze proudly.

"Oh, please," said Jessica.

Elizabeth scowled at her sister's cavalier attitude. *Does Jess have to be so cynical?* She wondered. She was still burning from her twin's accusations the night before that she'd been playing the role of teacher's pet. Elizabeth wasn't trying to be Kay's favorite—how could she help it if she was the best student?

"OK. Here's the deal," Kay started. "You have until Thursday night to reach the pickup point at Desert Oasis, which is nothing more than a diner, gas station, and convenience store.

"We've packed four days' worth of food and some first-aid supplies for each of you to carry in your backpack. You can fill your canteens over at the spigot by the bathrooms—keep drinking, but make it last. You won't get to a water supply today, but you can factor it into your route sometime tomorrow.

"And remember, even though it looks clean and fresh, don't drink water without first purifying it. With all the bacteria going around, it's too risky. You can't afford for anyone in the group to get sick. I've packed the water purifier in Elizabeth's pack."

Elizabeth forced herself not to react when she saw Jessica rib Ken and roll her eyes.

"That's fine, Kay," Elizabeth said, shooting Jessica a dirty look.

"Good. Why don't you go ahead and look through your packs," said Kay. "If you have questions about anything, just ask."

"What's this?" Jessica asked, pulling a pouch from her pack.

"Lunch," Brad answered. "Freeze-dried chicken and vegetables."

"Sounds delish," Jessica said, wrinkling her nose. "Looks like I'll be losing some weight the next few days."

"That reminds me," Kay interrupted. "Be sure to eat every meal. You may not feel hungry, especially in the middle of the day when it gets really hot. But you'll need all the calories and nutrients. And you'll get used to the freeze-dried taste. You might even start liking it—I do."

"I think I'll stick to California cuisine," Heather said dryly.

"And my first stop when we get back home is the Dairi Burger," Todd commented, pulling some dried fruit out of his pack.

"Enough about food," Brad said. "I want to make sure you understand the most important aspects of this trip. As we discussed back in Sweet Valley this weekend, over the next four days you'll not only learn about yourselves, you'll learn how to work with others. And you might as well get used to it, because for the rest of your life you'll be faced with having to deal with people you'd rather not have anything to do with."

Jessica took one look at Heather and knew exactly what Brad was talking about.

"Learn how to find the strengths in each other that will help the whole group," Kay continued. "Sometimes you'll need to take a step back when you know there's someone else in the group more able than you," she said, looking at all of them.

Jessica couldn't help but notice her sister looking straight at her. She rolled her eyes again. This adventure trek was the kind of thing Elizabeth loved, and she was acting more goody-goody than ever. Elizabeth had always been a nerd, but her

14

self-righteous attitude was really beginning to drive Jessica crazy. *I'm not going to let it get to me,* she decided, looking over at Heather. *I've got to focus all my tolerance where it's truly needed.*

Brad was talking now. "We've assigned each of you a buddy. Things may get a little hairy out there sometimes, and it's important to have someone who's responsible for your safety."

Jessica squeezed Ken's hand. Brad and Kay were sure to have noticed their special bond.

"Jessica, we've assigned you and Todd to be buddies," Brad announced.

"Are you serious?" Jessica couldn't believe her ears. "You must have made a mistake."

"No mistake," Kay said.

Jessica was beside herself. *This is just perfect. For the most boring trip in the universe, I've been assigned the most boring person on earth.*

Brad glanced at his list. "Elizabeth, you're with Bruce. And, Heather, you're with Ken."

Jessica gasped. Was this some cruel joke?

"Oh, Ken, we're buddies!" Heather bubbled, casting a triumphant look in Jessica's direction. "We're going to have so much fun looking at— oops, I mean looking after—each other."

Watching Heather bat her eyelashes at Ken, Jessica couldn't believe she'd be so brazen. Of course, Heather was never one to be subtle. *Ken . . . with Heather!* Jessica thought disgustedly. *I might as well have spent this week sitting in a bath of hot coals—that would have been fun compared to the torture this is going to be.*

"Do you really think these are the best matches for the group, Kay?" Elizabeth suddenly asked.

Jessica looked at her sister in surprise, until she realized that Elizabeth was probably pretty unhappy, too. She was matched up with Bruce Patman, the most arrogant person on the planet. *I'd rather be bored with Todd than have to listen to Bruce all day long,* Jessica figured.

"Yes, Elizabeth, we do," Kay answered. "We've put a great deal of thought into this and put you in these pairs for a reason."

Jessica felt a little bit of satisfaction when she saw her sister silenced. It looked as if being the teacher's pet didn't do her any good, after all.

"Kay and I have to take care of some last-minute details," Brad said. "Take a minute and relax—this'll be your last opportunity to do that for a while." Kay and Brad walked back over to the van, leaving the rest of them sitting at the table.

"I'm starting to feel better about this trip already," Heather said, grabbing Ken's hand. Ken laughed nervously and gently pulled away.

Elizabeth saw her sister fume and had to admit that she sympathized with her. Elizabeth didn't approve of the way Heather operated, either. Although Jessica was one of the all-time champion schemers on earth, Elizabeth knew she had a good heart and would never be as devious and spiteful as Heather Mallone.

"I can't believe they're doing this," Todd whispered to Elizabeth. "This is going to be a true test

16

of your tolerance, being matched up with Bruce, and all."

"You're right. We're supposed to learn how to triumph in the face of adversity. Trying to stick to Bruce will be the ultimate adversity," Elizabeth said, shaking her head.

"Yeah, and *watching* you stick to Bruce will be the ultimate adversity for me," Todd added, looking sadly into her eyes.

Elizabeth returned his gaze and knew exactly what he was thinking. A little while back she and Bruce had found out Mrs. Wakefield and Mr. Patman had been college sweethearts. The shock of discovery had driven the unlikely pair together, until everything came crashing to an end when Todd had walked in on Bruce and Elizabeth in the Wakefield kitchen in a passionate embrace.

Any feelings she'd had for Bruce then, Elizabeth now chalked up to temporary insanity. She was attracted to guys who were honest, sensitive, modest, and kind—guys like Todd. Bruce was the polar opposite. And now she was going to have to spend every minute of every day hanging around Bruce.

Elizabeth thought back to the time when she'd actually been interested in Bruce. They *had* bonded for a short time. Was there any chance this trip would bring out the vulnerability and sensitivity he had let her see back then?

Her thoughts were interrupted when Bruce snarled, "Oh, great, I get to have Miss Camp Counselor breathing down my back for the next four days. I might as well have brought along my mother." He threw back his arm and tossed a pebble toward the road.

"Put a lid on it, Bruce," Todd said. Before Bruce could start in again, Kay and Brad emerged from the van and approached the table.

"OK, gang," Kay called. "We just called the weather station on the cell phone to confirm the weather forecast. It still stands. They're talking torrential downpours, flooding, high-velocity winds. This is real. You guys have got to make it to Desert Oasis by Thursday evening, or you're going to be stuck in the storm. And we can't promise that we'll be able to find you."

Elizabeth felt a knot of dread growing in her stomach.

"You have everything you need to make it just fine," Brad said. "As long as you stick to the plan, that is. Remember, this area was mined back in the great California Gold Rush of 1849, and there are still a few mine shafts standing. It may seem really cool to explore them, but it's extremely dangerous. They could collapse at any moment, especially if people climb around inside them."

"Now is your chance to rise above expectations: your own, your parents', your teachers'," said Kay. "Look around at each other and realize that this week these people are your team—your family."

Elizabeth looked from one member of her "family" to the other. She could tell that Bruce wasn't even paying attention—he was reading a magazine he'd pulled from his pack. Heather had her eyes glued on Ken and kept inching her way closer into his space. While Ken appeared to be intent on Kay's and Brad's words, Elizabeth sensed that he was distracted by the fact that Heather was edging up next to him. Jessica seemed too busy pouting to be thinking about the challenges ahead of them. And even Todd looked a little preoccupied. Elizabeth found herself worrying that her "family" was not up to the task at hand. Did Kay and Brad actually believe that they would pull together as a team?

"Well, we're out of here," Kay announced. She and Brad walked across the parking lot and climbed into the van. Kay started the engine and put the van into gear.

"Oh, yeah," she yelled out the window before driving off. "Have fun!" And then they were gone.

Elizabeth couldn't push away the terrible feeling in the pit of her stomach as she watched the van disappear down the dusty road. *Come back,* she wanted to say. *I can't carry this whole group alone. We'll be lucky to get out of Death Valley alive.*

Chapter 2

As the sound of the engine subsided, the van became no more than a white dot on the horizon.

This is it, Todd realized. *The adventure begins.* But the adventure seemed to be getting less appealing by the minute. First of all, he was stuck for four days with Jessica Wakefield. On top of that, he had to worry about Elizabeth rediscovering her old feelings for Bruce. This wasn't exactly his idea of a romantic getaway.

"Anybody need to make a pit stop?" asked Ken, getting up from the table.

"Good idea," Heather said, following him to the bathrooms.

"I'm getting provisions," said Bruce, heading over to the minimart.

Jessica sat glowering in silence. Todd decided to use the opportunity to take up the buddy subject with Elizabeth.

21

"You know, Liz," he started, "no one is out here to watch us—we could switch partners so we can be together. I hate to see you forced to put up with Bruce's stupidity for the next four days."

"I'm sure it won't be so bad once we get started," Elizabeth replied. "Bruce'll calm down and stop teasing so much once he realizes that I'm not going to grab his bait."

"But, still, the hike would be so much more fun if we could be together," Todd tried again, reaching across the table to take her hand.

"This trip isn't about *fun*, Todd," she said in a light, scolding tone. "We have our whole lives to be together. This is an opportunity for us to grow as individuals." With that Elizabeth patted his hand and got up, walking over to the pile of packs.

Todd watched her get engrossed in her task of examining the supplies in her pack, checking off her list one by one. *It's no use,* he concluded. *I'm stuck with Jessica.* The thought of dealing with Jessica's whining all day long made Todd wince.

He looked across the table at his partner. She looked just about as miserable as he felt. Suddenly Heather's high-pitched laugh rang out, and Todd saw Jessica shiver with fury. Then he had an idea. Knowing how much Jessica hated Heather, Todd realized she would do anything to split Heather and Ken apart.

"Jessica, you're looking pretty dejected," Todd said in a friendly tone. She raised her eyebrows but didn't respond, focusing her attention on the table.

He continued. "For some strange reason—which

I'll never understand—you always seem to be able to convince Elizabeth to do just about anything," Todd said to her quietly. "How about convincing her to switch partners? I can't seem to get past her wanting to play by the rules."

"So you get to be with your girlfriend, and I end up with Bruce? Thanks, but no thanks," Jessica snorted. "Believe it or not, I'd rather be with you."

"No, I wouldn't do that to you," Todd said ingratiatingly. "You can convince Bruce to switch with Ken. Word among the guys is that Bruce thinks Heather is hot, so that shouldn't be too hard."

Jessica considered this for a moment. It didn't take long for a smile to creep across her face.

"You're on!" she said, shaking Todd's hand. Together they approached Elizabeth, with Todd hanging back to let Jessica work her persuasive magic.

"Say, Liz," started Jessica in her sweetest voice. "I'm starting to think this week might really be fun."

"That's great, Jess," Elizabeth said, clipping her odometer to her belt.

"It's just that—" Her voice cracked. She stuck out her lower lip and looked down at her feet.

"What is it?" Elizabeth asked, a look of concern on her face.

"I'm really upset about Heather. You know how she has it in for me—she'll stop at nothing to make my life miserable. I'm afraid that her being matched up with Ken is going to ruin the experience for me."

"Don't be silly, Jess," Elizabeth said dismissively. "Ken's absolutely crazy about you. He'd never let Heather get in the way of your relationship."

"It's not that I'm worried that all of Heather's disgusting attempts at flirting will actually work on Ken. It's just that with Heather matched up with my boyfriend, she'll use all her energy to try to charm him, instead of working toward a common goal."

Jess is good, she's really good, Todd thought. He looked at Elizabeth expectantly.

"I'm sure Heather will quickly grow bored of flirting with Ken once she sees he isn't returning her advances," Elizabeth said.

"OK, Liz, I'll admit it," Jessica continued. "Even though I have absolute faith that Ken won't be taken in by Heather, just knowing that she's doing everything she can to steal him away will distract me from the purpose of this trip." Jessica met Todd's eyes behind Elizabeth's back and grinned.

"So why don't we do this," Jessica continued. "I'll switch partners with you so that you can be with Todd."

Elizabeth narrowed her eyes. "And you want to be partners with Bruce, I take it?"

"Now, wait a minute, I'm not done. Then I'll talk Bruce into switching with Ken, which should be a snap because he's got a thing for Heather, although for the life of me, I can't imagine why.

24

Anyway, everybody's happy. You and Todd get to be together, and Ken and I get to be together. And Heather and Bruce are free to go ahead and drive each other crazy."

Elizabeth didn't say anything for a minute. *What's her problem?* Todd wondered. Didn't she want to be his partner?

"I'm sorry, you guys, I just don't think it's a good idea," Elizabeth finally said, looking from Jessica to Todd. "Don't you remember how Brad and Kay said that a major part of the experience is learning how to get along with people you may not like? If we switch partners, we're sabotaging the whole point of the exercise."

"It's an exercise in stupidity, as far as I'm concerned," snapped Jessica. She stormed off to the bathroom.

Elizabeth looked at Todd but said nothing. Then she took off in the direction that Jessica had headed.

Todd watched her walk away and realized that she was beyond persuasion. Why did his girlfriend always have to be such a stickler about rules? He'd thought Elizabeth would jump at the chance to avoid Bruce and be with him instead.

Todd's mind wandered to a painful memory.

The afternoon sun cast a golden glow upon the bodies entwined in the Wakefields' kitchen. Bruce's long, muscular arms were wrapped tightly around the small of Elizabeth's back. Lifting her face to his, Elizabeth caught Todd's eye over Bruce's shoulder. She froze, her eyes proclaiming her guilt.

Try as he might, Todd couldn't get rid of the sickening visions. Maybe Elizabeth actually *wanted* to be stuck in the desert with Bruce.

"You kids going camping out there in the Valley?" Startled, Todd turned to see a gray-haired man dressed all in denim and wearing a bolo tie. He was sitting on a stool a few yards away in the shade of a fence. Where had he come from?

"Yes, sir, we are." The man nodded slowly, stroking the stubble on his cheeks. "Do you live around here?" Todd asked, trying to be friendly. The man turned, his bloodshot eyes examining Todd up and down.

"Mighty hot out there," the man drawled finally. "You best be careful."

Todd nodded, relieved the old guy didn't seem to be in the mood for conversation.

"Well, have a nice day," Todd said. The man cackled. A strange premonition made the hairs on the back of Todd's neck stand straight up. He knew this trip was going to give him a lot more to worry about than Bruce Patman making a move on Elizabeth. He could feel it.

Elizabeth walked out of the bathroom to see Todd and Jessica sulking by their packs. Heather was playing some sort of keep-away with Ken, and Bruce was sitting at the picnic table, reading a comic book. Why wasn't anyone doing something to get their trip started? Was she going to have to do everything?

"Well, I guess we'd better plot our day's jour-

26

ney," Elizabeth said, looking at her watch. "It's nine o'clock now. Figure we'll break for lunch at one, and get to tonight's camp by five. That way we'll have plenty of time to set up before sundown."

"Who died and left you in charge?" Bruce taunted, looking up from his comic book.

"I'm not taking charge, Bruce, but if we don't stop arguing about buddies and fooling around, we'll never get out of this gas station," she replied. She tried to ignore Todd's petulant look.

"Elizabeth's right, you guys," Ken agreed. "We're here now, and the van's long gone. So there's no use complaining. It's time we got serious about this."

"Thank you, Ken," said Elizabeth. "I'm just trying to get everyone started. We can all plan it together. Does anybody have a problem with what I've said so far? Lunch at one, camp at five?" She looked around at the others, waiting for someone to respond.

"Lunch at one? That sounds fine," Heather said at last. The others mumbled their approval.

"Good. Let's get out our maps and start plotting a course." *At least someone in our group is using her brain. I haven't heard one of you lay out a plan,* Elizabeth thought, doing her best to contain her frustration.

"Didn't Kay and Brad tell us that it works best to have one person at a time responsible for navigation?" Ken asked.

"Oh, right," Elizabeth said. She wanted to be the navigator, for the first day at least, but she didn't want the others to think she was being bossy. "Does anybody want to volunteer to plot our trail and make sure we stick to it?" she asked the group.

"I volunteer Elizabeth Wakefield," said Bruce.

"Yeah, Elizabeth, you were the one paying the most attention during that part of the lesson. Why don't you do it today?" Todd seconded.

Elizabeth forced herself to hide her satisfaction. "I'd be fine with that, if no one objects," she said nonchalantly.

Jessica shrugged.

"As long as I don't have to do it," Heather said. "All that latitude, longtitude, and angle stuff was a complete bore, wasn't it, Ken?"

"Actually, Heather, I kind of liked it," he answered. "But it's fine with me if Liz wants to navigate today."

"OK. Give me a few minutes to chart the course."

While the others filled their canteens, Elizabeth pulled a pencil and paper from her pack and spread the map out on the table. Scanning the diagram, she spotted the symbol that identified an underground spring. They'd need to get there by the following night. She followed the line that led to the spring and measured off ten miles. *We'll want to start off slow,* she thought. *If today's hike seems easy, we can always push ourselves to go farther tomorrow. I don't want everyone to be exhausted on our first day—I'd never hear the end of it.*

"You guys, I figured it out," Elizabeth called.

"You want to see the trail I've laid out?"

Everyone came over to look at the map.

"This is where we are, and this is Desert Oasis, about thirty-five miles away if you draw a straight line. But since we'll have to cross this mountain ridge to get there"—she pointed to a spot on the map—"I figure that will add at least five miles to our trek. And since we'll be climbing, that will slow us down. But it's completely manageable," she said, echoing Brad's reassuring words.

She looked up and held her breath, waiting for one of them to argue or complain. Heather blew a lock of hair off her face and shrugged. Bruce took a swig of water. Jessica picked at one of her fingernails. *I guess I impressed them with my logic,* Elizabeth thought.

"Everyone ready?" she said out loud.

"Ready as I'll ever be," grumbled Jessica.

"Ken, would you be a dear and help me with my pack?" Heather asked in a sugarcoated voice.

"Ummm, sure, Heather." Ken lifted her pack so she could slip her arms under the straps.

"Don't you go getting any ideas, Wakefield," said Bruce. "It's your pack to carry, your pack to lift."

"No problem, Bruce. I wasn't even going to ask," Elizabeth responded cheerfully as she whisked her pack onto her back. It was heavier than she'd expected. She felt her knees buckle a bit but caught herself before anyone noticed. "No sweat," she said, adopting a casual pose.

Todd looked at Jessica, but before he could

offer his help she said, "Forget it, Wilkins, I'm strong enough to lift my own pack, thank you very much." She heaved it onto her back and glared at Heather. Heather just smiled. The guys all put on their packs and looked to Elizabeth to start them off.

Elizabeth took a second to orient herself, looking first down at her compass and then up over the flat expanse of dirt. Far-off mountains loomed like shadows, their tops glistening with snow.

Elizabeth tried to imagine what the first people who'd found this place must have thought when they'd been confronted with its enormity. She remembered learning about the early gold prospectors who'd traveled across these very plains and canyons. Many had died from dehydration and overexposure, giving Death Valley its ominous name. Elizabeth shivered.

After a few moments she shook her head. Dwelling on the terrors of Death Valley would only make her crazy.

"Let's go," she said out loud. Elizabeth moved to the front of the group and took her first step away from the gas station—the last evidence of the civilization they were leaving behind.

"Can you believe that someone would have the nerve to litter here?" Elizabeth cried, spotting a candy wrapper tangled in some sagebrush. Crouching down, she noticed dots of color winking through the dry foliage. "Look at these perfect little wildflowers hiding here," she exclaimed,

30

leaning closer to examine the brilliant yellow, orange, and red blossoms.

"Don't fall!" Bruce jeered, giving Elizabeth a gentle nudge with his leg as he passed her. Falling into the brush, Elizabeth was stung immediately by sharp pricklers.

"Ouch!" Red welts forming on her arms, Elizabeth looked at Bruce's figure striding ahead of her on the trail. She'd told herself that she was going to do her best to get along with Bruce, but if he insisted on being such a jerk, there was nothing she could do.

Brushing herself off, Elizabeth wondered if she should have taken Jessica and Todd up on their offer to switch buddies. Then she remembered how adamant she was about keeping to the letter of Brad and Kay's instructions. *No, this will be good for me*, she decided.

Still, she looked longingly over her shoulder at Todd, who was walking silently behind a chattering Jessica. It was going to be a lonely four days.

But at least the solitude would give her ample time to do a lot of thinking. Part of the experience was to write in journals every night, something Elizabeth did anyway. She was planning to turn her journal entries into an article for the school paper. And if it was good enough, she'd try to get it published in the *Sweet Valley News*.

Then she had an exciting thought—maybe SVSS would hire her to do some promotional writing. They'd been working to expand their organization, and she could get in on the ground floor.

Then she could get to know Kay even better, she realized happily. In better spirits now, Elizabeth hiked with a spring in her step.

Before she knew it, the sun had moved up in the sky and her scalp was starting to burn. *Good thing I remembered to bring something to cover my head,* she thought as she took a white baseball cap out of her side pocket and put it on. She pulled her ponytail out of the back of the cap, adjusting its brim to keep the sun out of her eyes.

"You guys! Hold up! It's time for lunch!" Heather called out from behind. *Already?* Elizabeth thought, looking at her watch. Sure enough, it was one o'clock on the button. *Heather must have been watching the clock.*

"Is everyone hungry? Or do you think we should push ourselves a little farther?" she asked the group.

"I think we should stick to the schedule you so carefully laid out," Heather said defiantly.

"Fine, I was just asking," Elizabeth quickly said, not wanting to create a fuss. *As long as everyone stays fed, they'll be less likely to get irritable later,* she figured.

The members of the group wriggled out of their packs.

"Oh, gross! My T-shirt is soaked with sweat!" Jessica squealed, feeling her back.

"It is pretty hot," Todd said, wiping his face with a rag. "I guess we're not going to get much shade today."

"No, today's hike should be pretty barren, by

the looks of the map. I think we'll reach some trees tomorrow, though." Elizabeth searched through her pack for the day's lunch.

"You brought a TV?" Bruce exclaimed incredulously.

Elizabeth looked up to see Heather pulling a mini-TV from her backpack.

"You don't expect me to miss my show, do you?" Heather asked.

"Heather! We were specifically instructed not to bring anything that would enable us to communicate with the outside world," Elizabeth scolded.

"I'm not interested in the outside world," Heather answered, unconcerned. "From one o'clock to two o'clock I'm interested in the world of Sea Haven, the locale of *Sunrise, Sunset*." She turned on her TV and fussed with the antenna. "Shoot. The reception out here's terrible."

Jessica looked at Heather with disbelief. She knew Heather was spoiled rotten, but she couldn't believe the girl would actually have the nerve to bring a TV along on a survival trek!

"Why do you watch that show, anyway?" Ken asked Heather.

If Ken hasn't been thoroughly repulsed by Heather already, he's sure to be disgusted with this display of stupidity, Jessica thought with relief.

"The people on this show are like my friends. Besides, soap operas teach a lot about life, about relationships," Heather explained earnestly.

"Right—I hear they're piping daytime soaps

into classrooms as educational programming," Jessica quipped sarcastically.

"Don't tell me you've never watched soaps, Wakefield," Heather responded.

"Once, and when I finally stopped gagging, I decided never to watch them again." Actually, Jessica used to watch lots of soaps, but she didn't want Ken to know.

"That's not true, Jess. Remember how you used to tape *Days of Turmoil* so that you could watch it when you got home from school?" Elizabeth asked.

Jessica threw her an angry glare. "That was ages ago. And it didn't take me long to realize that my own life is much more interesting than anything some stupid Hollywood writer could dream of," she said, smiling brightly at Ken. To her annoyance he was helping Heather fiddle with the antenna.

Bruce laughed. "Your life is a regular thriller. I can't wait to see the TV miniseries: *Jessica, Her Boring Life and Loves*."

"Oh, shut up, Bruce," Jessica said. With all her spiteful energy directed at Heather, she couldn't think of a clever comeback.

"So who's Brian, and why doesn't Claire want her sister to go out with him?" Ken asked suddenly.

Jessica looked over at Ken and almost did a double take. He was actually watching Heather's soap!

"Oh, Brian is this guy who came into Claire's life when she was a drug addict—"

"Do you mind? We're trying to eat," snarled Jessica.

"Fine, we'll just move away from you guys so we can watch the show in peace." Unbelievably, Ken followed Heather a few feet away and plopped down next to her.

I must be dreaming, thought Jessica. *What kind of poison has Heather been giving Ken to make him act so weird? And where can I find the antidote?*

"I think this is it, but I'm not sure," Elizabeth declared, checking her map for the fourth time.

"Even if it isn't, it looks like a fine place to me," Jessica said, tugging at her shoulder straps. They'd been walking all afternoon in the hot sun, and she couldn't wait to rip off her pack and collapse. The thought of lying on the dirty ground didn't even put a damper on her desire to rest her body. She massaged an aching hip.

"Yeah, Liz, I think it's time to stop," Todd added, sounding a little impatient.

"OK, OK. I just wanted to make sure we'd reached today's goal," Elizabeth said, loosening the belt of her pack. "If we get thrown off course now, we'll have to make up for it tomorrow."

"Yeah, yeah, we know, General Wakefield," Bruce said, tossing his pack onto the ground. "That's what we've got you around for, to keep us in line."

"Now, that's not fair," Elizabeth said defensively.

"Calm down, Liz. After a whole day with Bruce, haven't you learned how to block out the sound of his voice? That's what I do," Jessica said.

"Very funny, Wakefield."

"Stop it, you guys," Ken said firmly. "Elizabeth, we really do appreciate the way you're being so diligent about the navigation."

A little too diligent, Jessica would have liked to add. Usually, Jessica appreciated having someone as reliable as Elizabeth for a sister. She often counted on Elizabeth to keep her on schedule— promptness was not one of Jessica's attributes.

But right now Elizabeth was really starting to annoy Jessica with her fastidiousness. One whole day of watching Heather hang all over her boyfriend was hard enough, without having Elizabeth constantly harping on the value of this experience.

And Ken! Ken wasn't even pushing Heather away! Kay and Brad had said this would be a learning experience. But all Jessica was learning was just how much of a back-stabbing little vermin Heather was. And that her own boyfriend was spineless! *What's the value in that?* she wondered.

"Thank you for that vote of confidence, Ken," Elizabeth said. "I know we're all tired, and that's why we're cranky," she said, looking pointedly at Todd.

"You're calling me cranky?" Todd asked.

"Welllll—"

"Darn right I'm cranky. It's as hot as a desert in this here Death Valley!" he said, laughing. Elizabeth and Ken laughed, too.

Even Jessica had to chuckle at Todd's goofiness—anything to relieve her rising tension. She flopped down onto her pack and took stock of the camp Elizabeth had found. The clearing was shaded by a small hill on one side and flanked by a line of cacti on the other.

"Let's get our camp set up. I think we should build the fire right here," Elizabeth said, brushing clear an area with her foot.

"Hold it right there, Wakefield," interrupted Bruce. "Building a fire is a man's job."

"Maybe in the Stone Age, where you're from, Bruce. In this country we like to think that women and men are equally capable of building fires, and lots of other things," Elizabeth said hotly, staring Bruce down with her hands planted firmly on her hips.

"Hey, hey, Liz," said Todd gently, coming up behind Elizabeth and rubbing her shoulders. "Bruce was just being Bruce. You don't have to prove yourself to us. You've done enough today— how 'bout you build the fire tomorrow?"

"I am pretty exhausted," she conceded. "I wouldn't mind a rest."

"That's a good girl, Liz, give yourself a break," Todd said. "I'll help Bruce build the fire."

Watching her sister collapse onto the dirt reminded Jessica to get started blowing up her air mattress. She pulled it out from her pack.

"While you guys are doing that, Ken and I will start getting the meal together. I think chili is on the menu tonight!" chimed Heather.

Elizabeth lifted her head. "That would be great, you guys. And after we eat, there should be plenty of time to write in our journals before it gets too dark."

Jessica groaned. *First I have to watch that rat play house with my boyfriend, and then I have to write about it?* She blew into her air mattress with so much force, she thought her eyes would pop out of her head.

"OK, everybody, soup's on!" sang Heather, licking her finger after dipping it into the pot of chili that was perched over the fire. "Ken, you hold the pot and I'll serve."

Jessica was so hungry, she thought she could have eaten the whole pot. But watching Ken follow Heather around in a circle, holding the pot while she ladled out the chili, took her appetite away. By the time the two came over to serve her, the sight of the chili made her sick to her stomach.

"I don't want too much," she said when Heather bent over to fill her bowl.

"Yeah, I guess you have put on a couple of pounds," Heather said with a sneer, straightening up to eye Jessica's seated figure.

"I have *not* put on *any* pounds. I'm just not hungry!" Jessica felt her chest heave with anger.

"Jess, you really should eat. You need to keep up your strength for the hike tomorrow," Ken said warmly.

Not as much strength as I need to hold myself back from ripping every single hair out of Heather Mallone's head, Jessica thought glumly as Heather silently spooned her a huge portion.

"Eat up, Jess," Heather crowed.

Without thinking, Jessica stuffed a huge spoonful into her mouth. Immediately the hot chili burned her tongue. "Ouch!" she cried through her mouthful of food. Gulping down some cool water, she decided that as soon as they were done eating, it was time to have a little talk with Ken.

"Ken, could I talk to you for a minute?" Jessica asked after cleaning her now-empty bowl.

"Sure, Jess, what's up?"

"I mean *alone*," she implored, gesturing for Ken to follow her.

"Don't go too far, you guys," Elizabeth warned. "Remember how cold it gets in the desert."

"We got it, we got it," said Jessica, weary of her sister's caretaking.

When they were a few yards away from the rest of the group, Jessica sat down and patted the ground next to her. Ken sat down close beside her.

"What's wrong, Jess?" he asked.

"I just wanted to be alone with you for a minute." Jessica took Ken's hand, threading her fingers through his. "I've been missing you all day. Haven't you missed me?"

"Sure, I have. What do you think?"

"I don't know, Ken. You seem to be ignoring me." Jessica pouted a little, just to prove her point.

"Ignoring you? That's ridiculous. It's not my fault that I have to hang around Heather all day," he said.

"That's just it. You don't seem to mind hanging around that poor excuse for a human being."

Ken chuckled. "That's a little harsh, Jess. I'm just trying to make the best of the situation." He

39

put an arm around her shoulder and drew her close to him. "You should, too," he added.

"But she's being such an outrageous flirt—haven't you noticed?" Jessica could barely contain her anger, even with the gentle warmth of Ken's arm circling her shoulders.

"Yeah, I guess she's a flirt. But it's harmless. You're not jealous, are you?" he asked, giving her a squeeze.

Jessica paused. "Maybe just a little."

"You, jealous? I don't believe it!"

"Well, I am."

"Jess, you're being silly. You should know by now how wild I am about you." He brushed Jessica's cheek with a light kiss.

"I do, Ken, I do. It's just that Heather—I don't know—she makes me a little crazy. You understand that, don't you?" Jessica met Ken's eyes. "After all she's done to me?"

Ken nodded. "Listen to me, Jess," he said, taking both her hands in his. "I'm in love with you, and no one is going to change that. Especially not Heather."

They kissed deeply, and Jessica felt all of Ken's love washing over her. She didn't want the kiss to stop, ever. How could she have doubted the depth of Ken's love for her? And why would he ever be attracted to phony Heather Mallone when he had Jessica Wakefield's lips to kiss?

Suddenly Elizabeth's voice rang out over the desert. "Ken! Jess! Where are you guys? It's getting dark!"

"Ignore her, Ken," Jessica cooed when she felt Ken stiffen. "Let's stay here a little while longer—I'm not done with you yet." She wrapped her arms tighter around him.

"No, we'd better get back." He pulled himself from her embrace. "I'm not too anxious to encounter any of Death Valley's nocturnal hunters. We'll be safer if we stay near the fire." He reached out a hand for Jessica to grab. "Besides, we still have to write in our journals."

Reluctantly, Jessica took Ken's outstretched hand and pulled herself up. *The last thing I want to do right now is write in some stupid journal,* she thought. *There goes Elizabeth again, messing up my life.*

Chapter 3

Elizabeth's Journal
Death Valley Adventure Trek
Day 1

Well, day number one of the Sweet Valley High adventure trek has come to a close. Luckily, the group seems none the worse for the wear. I was really worried for a while, but I guess everyone realized that when the van disappeared on the horizon, there was no turning back.

Actually, the minute the van disappeared, Todd and Jessica came running to me like little babies. I can't believe they teamed up against me to try to get us to switch partners. Jessica's childish behavior isn't really out of character—I should know. But the fact that Todd was whining about wanting to be paired with me instead of Jessica was rather surprising. He's always saying that he wants us to be able to function apart as well as we function together. I thought he had more pride than to ask for Jessica's help in his scheme to keep me away from Bruce. I wish they would at least try to comprehend the full meaning of this experience.

Hiking ten miles today wasn't too bad. I'll admit, I had been a little concerned about being able to keep up with the others. With all of their cheerleading practices, Jess and Heather work out all the time. The basketball and football teams keep Todd and Ken in tip-top shape. And Bruce gets a lot of exercise on the tennis team. But I spend more time exercising my brain than my body. Thank goodness, it seems to be holding up just fine. Good genes, I guess—thanks, Mom and Dad.

I can't get over the beauty of the desert. It's so quiet, you can almost hear the silence. The cacti and other plant life are rather stark, but there are also thousands of tiny wildflowers. Poppies are everywhere. And the air is incredibly clean.

I hope tomorrow goes as smoothly as today. Smoother! Maybe I can even coerce Bruce into having a real conversa-

tion with me. No, I'd better not set my sights too high. If we can make it through the day without Jessica and Heather ripping each other to shreds, I'll be happy.

Bruce's Journal
Death Valley Adventure Trek
Day 1

What a huge, stupid waste of time. I can't believe I'm stuck in the desert with this bunch of geeks. At least I get to miss school. If they only knew how ridiculous this is, they'd never have excused us all from class. What's the big deal? So we hike a few days in the hot sun and sleep outside at night. It's not like we're navigating on the ocean, or anything. Or climbing a huge mountain. Where's all the risk and danger they kept talking about?

I am learning how much cooler I am than the rest of this bunch. Even Heather. What a disappointment she's turning out to be. I thought maybe we could hook up—it would definitely break up the monotony of this trip. But she's drooling all over Matthews. And he's being a complete loser. He actually watched that stupid TV show with her! Some guys have no self-respect. What a wuss. I can't believe I'm actually writing this stuff. Who needs to write when you can afford a secretary?

Heather's Journal
Death Valley Adventure Trek
Day 1

This is going better than if I had planned it myself. The gods must have been smiling down on me to get Ken and me assigned as buddies. Now I get to kill two birds with one stone: make Ken Matthews fall in love with me and make Jessica Wakefield suffer miserably. I love watching that spoiled brat huff and puff with jealousy as I wrap Ken around my little pinkie.

I must say, Ken is falling prey to my charms without a struggle. It's almost too easy. I might enjoy a bit more of a challenge. Maybe I'll move on to Todd once I've got Ken snagged. Now, that would be a coup! Not one but two Wakefield boyfriends stolen out from under their perky little noses!

I don't understand why they made this survival thing into such a big deal. Aside from feeling really grimy after four days in this heat and dirt, it'll be painless. And the dry air is great for my complexion. I'll return to Sweet Valley in rare form, with one of the hottest guys in school snapping at my heels. Maybe even two!

Ken's Journal
Death Valley Adventure Trek
Day 1

Jess sure shocked me tonight. She's always been so self-confident, I can't believe she'd be jealous about my spending time with another girl. Heather is really pretty, with a good sense of humor and everything, but one girl is all I can handle at a time. And Jessica Wakefield is more than enough for any guy to manage!

I wish she wouldn't be so sensitive. I know she believes Heather is out to get her, but I don't think Heather is seriously trying to steal me away from Jess. Just seeing that last sentence written down makes it seem completely ridiculous. Why would Heather do that? And why doesn't Jess trust me enough to know I wouldn't fall for it?

Aside from Jess being paranoid, from the looks of things, this trip shouldn't be too bad. I wouldn't mind a little more challenge, in fact. I was kind of looking forward to discovering some new strengths in myself. I think tomorrow I'd like to take responsibility for navigation.

Jessica's Journal
Death Valley Adventure Trek
Day 1

If I didn't have baby pictures of Liz and me in Mom's arms at the hospital, I'd think she was put on this earth by aliens. She's so unreal! I don't think there's another human being on this planet as straitlaced as she is! She was so dense about switching buddies. This is our adventure, not Kay and Brad's. We're supposed to be left to our own devices, not follow the letter of the law. That's what we have school for. Now Ken is being pulled right out from under my nose. And it's all Liz's fault!

Speaking of Heather. I can't even think of the words to write about her, she makes me so mad. Anything I could put on paper would make this journal burn right up.

This stupid, stupid trip. I can't believe I'm doing this. It's not like it's even hard or anything. What a catastrophe!

Todd's Journal
Death Valley Adventure Trek
Day 1

Sometimes I wish my girlfriend would lighten up. She just gets too carried away about things. Like this trip. I mean, for all her talking about what a growing, learning experience this will be, I think it's just going to be four days of walking around in the hot sun.

Except that I have to walk around with Jessica and watch Elizabeth with Bruce. I wish Liz wasn't so stubborn about the buddy thing. I know it happened a long time ago, and I believe Liz when she says her feelings for Bruce are totally gone.

But my stomach kept churning all day, seeing them together again. It looked like they didn't interact much today, but they're going to be spending so much time together, they have to start talking at some point. What if Bruce turns on the charm? What if Liz starts reminiscing about how the invulnerable Bruce Patman opened up to her? She's bound to try to get him to open up again. What if he does? What if she starts liking him better than me? He is richer and better looking. How can I compete with him?

I can't believe I just wrote that. I've got to get over this insecurity. Bruce is a jerk and always will be a jerk. I shouldn't let him get to me.

Chapter 4

"Mind if I sleep next to you, cutie?"

At the sound of Todd's voice Elizabeth looked up from her journal. Todd, dressed in fuzzy red flannel pajamas, looked down at her with his eyebrows raised slightly and his head tilted to one side. The mere sight of him gave Elizabeth a warm glow throughout her body. She completely forgot that she'd just been writing about how annoyed she was at him.

"I can't think of anyone I'd rather be sleeping next to," she said, giving him a welcoming smile as she snapped her journal shut and stood up from her seat on a rock. She circled her hand around the back of his neck and whispered into his ear. "Let's sleep a little bit away from the rest of the group. We can pretend we're all alone."

He looked at her with shining eyes and grinned. "One of these days we're going to have to go on a camping trip all by ourselves," murmured Todd after they were settled in their sleeping bags, lying side by side, facing each other.

"Most definitely," agreed Elizabeth, admiring the way the firelight reflected the blond and gold strands in Todd's brown hair. *He's the cutest guy in the world,* she thought fondly.

Todd reached a hand out to brush a strand of hair off Elizabeth's forehead. He leaned in to kiss her nose. Then her mouth, her neck, her ears. Elizabeth giggled with delight.

"Oh, gross," Bruce snarled, ruining the moment. "Could you save your drooling and panting for another time?"

Elizabeth reluctantly pulled away from Todd's embrace. Bruce was leering at them from his sleeping bag on the other side of the fire.

Jessica and Ken were in a huddle, whispering and in their sleeping bags. Heather, dressed in a cotton lace nightie, was spreading out her sleeping bag right next to Ken's.

"Are you going for a threesome, Heather?" asked Bruce. Jessica turned her head and saw Heather.

"Heather, what do you think you're doing?" she demanded.

"I'm just setting up a place to sleep," Heather said, smoothing the corners of her sleeping bag over her air mattress.

"Could you sleep somewhere else?" asked Jessica, sitting up.

"Like where? I have to be near the fire—this is the only open spot."

"Bruce has a big empty spot next to him," Jessica said.

"I dare anyone to sleep near me," Bruce said, laughing. "I thrash and kick all night."

"It's OK, Heather, you can sleep here. I've got plenty of room," Ken said.

Heather scooted into her sleeping bag with a smile on her face.

"Oops! I'm sorry, Ken—I didn't mean to kick you." Heather giggled.

Elizabeth saw Jessica frown, but she couldn't hear the words her sister was mumbling.

What's that brick doing in my bed? Half awake, Elizabeth tried to roll away from whatever was pressing into her spine, only to have something sharp pierce her hip.

"Owww!" she said out loud, waking herself up. It took her a second to realize she wasn't back in her bed at home. Rubbing her eyes, Elizabeth lifted herself on her elbow and saw five sleeping bodies sprawled around a campfire site, which was now a crackling pile of glowing orange embers. *Oh, yeah, I'm in Death Valley.*

She sat up and felt every muscle ache. Maybe she shouldn't have laughed when Jessica had packed her air mattress. Looking up, Elizabeth gasped at the vision that faced her. Streaks of pink, yellow, and red splashed across the sky. Bands of wispy lavender clouds sailed overhead, their undersides glowing gold—evidence of the sun hiding just behind the horizon. Elizabeth gulped

53

in the sight, the air crisp and cold in her nostrils.

Glancing over at Todd's sleeping head, her first impulse was to wake him. Then she thought again. Even though Todd was more sensitive than most boys, he didn't appreciate things like beautiful sunrises as much as Elizabeth did—he'd probably just be annoyed that she'd woken him. With a pang she thought of her best friend, Enid Rollins. *Enid would love this. I really wish she'd been chosen for this trip instead of Heather.*

Elizabeth lay back in her sleeping bag to watch the sun rise in the sky. After a few peaceful moments her eyes fluttered shut, the image of the glorious morning still vivid behind her closed lids.

The next thing she knew, Elizabeth felt someone shake her.

"Liz, are you awake?" It was Todd's voice. She opened her eyes to see Todd crouching over her.

"I guess I fell back asleep," she said sleepily. "Oh, Todd, I saw the most extraordinary sunrise this morning. It was breathtaking!"

"Oh, really? That's nice." Todd buried his face in her long hair. "I think you're pretty breathtaking, too."

Elizabeth smiled to herself, glad she hadn't woken him. She wrapped her arms around his neck and gave him a kiss on the forehead.

"Good morning to you, too!" He laughed, slipping out of her grasp. "You'd better get moving, sleepyhead—everybody else is awake." He gave her a quick peck on the lips and got up to stoke the fire.

54

Elizabeth sat up to check on everyone else. Bruce was leaning against a juniper tree, brushing his teeth. Ken was over at the backpacks, looking at the map, and Jessica was sitting on her sleeping bag, tugging at the knots in her long blond hair. Heather was the only one still in her sleeping bag.

"Jeez! It's freezing!" Heather screamed suddenly, burrowing deep into her bag.

"Maybe if you hadn't worn that skimpy nightgown, you wouldn't be so cold," Jessica, who was wearing her flannel pajamas, commented.

Maybe if you hadn't listened to me and had brought the silk nightshirt you'd originally packed, you'd be freezing, too, Elizabeth thought, grinning to herself.

"Ken, would you be a sweetie and get a sweatshirt out of my pack?" Heather asked.

"Sure, Heather," Ken said. After a moment of digging through her pack, he pulled out a lavender sweatshirt.

"This OK?"

"Perfect! Hurry—I don't want to catch pneumonia."

Ken delivered the sweatshirt to Heather's outstretched arms.

"Ahhhh," Heather said, pulling the thick sweatshirt over her head. "Help me up?" She held out her hand, and Ken pulled her up. Suddenly she lost her balance and fell into Ken, who held out his arms to brace her.

"Whoops!" She giggled.

"Oh, brother!" Elizabeth heard Jessica mutter

under her breath. Elizabeth crawled out of her sleeping bag, feeling her joints creak. *Next time I do this, I'm* definitely *bringing an air mattress,* she thought.

"Is anyone hungry?" Todd asked. "We've got hot oatmeal, hot cocoa, and cold Pop-Tarts."

"I'm starving!" Elizabeth responded. They all gathered around the campfire and munched on their breakfast.

After they'd eaten, Ken pulled over the map.

"I've figured out today's hike," he announced.

"You did? Already?" Elizabeth asked. She had just assumed she'd be navigator the whole trip.

"Yeah. You were asleep and I figured you wouldn't mind. I paid pretty good attention during that lecture, too."

"Oh, that's totally OK, Ken." Elizabeth shrugged. "It's not like it was my job or anything."

"Yeah, Liz, you're not the only responsible one in the group," Jessica called, folding her air mattress into a small square.

"I never said that," Elizabeth said. "I'm happy to let someone else take over that responsibility." *It's great that Ken is sharing some of my enthusiasm about this trip,* she told herself.

"Piece of cake," Bruce stated after Ken showed them the day's journey of twelve miles over relatively flat terrain.

"Looks easy enough," agreed Todd.

Even Elizabeth had all but forgotten the sense of foreboding she'd felt the day before. Buckling the waist belt of her pack, she realized she was even getting used to the heavy weight on her back.

Ken and Heather set the pace in front as they took off.

The ground was hard and brittle and covered with loose rocks and gravel. Elizabeth was glad she was wearing hiking boots—the last thing she needed was to twist an ankle. But at least the sun wasn't ferocious.

"Nice that it's not so hot yet, isn't it?" Elizabeth said to Bruce after a few minutes.

"Hmmmph," he grunted. Elizabeth, wondering why she even bothered, decided to give up trying to connect with Bruce.

The group moved along smoothly as the heat of the day rose with the sun.

All of a sudden Heather stopped and grabbed her heel. "I think I'm getting a blister," she whined, leaning on Ken.

"Gee, Heather, maybe you should have thought about that before you decided to wear those impractical shoes," Jessica called out.

Elizabeth silently agreed. *I can't believe I'm thinking this, but Jess was right—even Lila would have been a better choice than Heather for this trip.*

"I'm starving. Todd, do you know what time it is?" Jessica asked, knowing full well that he wasn't wearing a watch.

"I have no idea."

"It must be time for lunch. Ken! Hold on!" Jessica yelled, trotting up the dusty path. Pushing Heather aside, Jessica grabbed Ken's wrist and peered at his watch. "We're all starving, it's got to be time for lunch."

"Let me figure out where we are," Ken said, pulling his hand from Jessica's grasp so that he could unfold the map and check his compass. Jessica watched his eyes darken with concentration. She felt a rush of affection for her boyfriend, even though he hadn't responded to her touch the way she would have liked.

"I think I see something ahead," called Bruce, who'd continued down the path. "Looks like a mine shaft." Jessica and the others ran to catch up with him. Bruce was right; a wooden archway was built into the side of a hill. Bruce stood at the entrance, peering into the dark tunnel. "Let's check it out!"

"Bruce, don't you remember what Kay and Brad said about the mine shafts? They could collapse at any time!" Elizabeth said.

"I know, Mother, dear. I'm just getting a closer look." Bruce circled the opening of the mine shaft, pushing at the splintered beams to test their strength.

"Well, we might as well stop here for lunch. It seems about right," Ken decided.

Heather looked at her watch. "Perfect!" She walked over to the shade of a juniper tree and pulled her TV out of her backpack.

"Great timing, Matthews," said Bruce over his shoulder. "We wouldn't want you to miss your favorite soap."

"Give me a break, Bruce."

They all sat down to eat. Then, to Jessica's horror, Ken got up and planted himself next to Heather and her TV.

"Hold on, you guys, listen to this!" Heather said suddenly. She turned up the volume so they could hear.

"We interrupt your regular programming to give you a news flash. This just in: The California correctional authorities from the state penitentiary in Red Canyon Creek have put the area in high alert. Three dangerous convicts have escaped the prison. State officials are warning people in the area to watch out for these three men."

Jessica shivered as three mug shots flashed across the tiny screen.

"If you have any information regarding these fugitives, please call the number you see on the screen immediately. We now return to your scheduled programming."

Heather turned off the TV before *Sunrise, Sunset* resumed.

"That was the prison we passed on the way here!" she cried. "What if the fugitives are here? What if we run into them?" Heather looked as if she'd seen a ghost—her skin was ashen, and her pupils had grown deep and dark.

"It *was* really close to where we were dropped off," Elizabeth said thoughtfully. "I remember seeing the prison too."

"Yeah, and they're not going to head straight into town where they could be caught," Todd added, looking worried.

"What're we going to do? We're totally vulnerable!" Heather let out a whimper.

"I hardly think that escaped convicts would head straight for the desert in their first moments of freedom," Jessica said, rolling her eyes. *She* wasn't going to act all skittish.

"Don't worry, Heather," soothed Ken. "Think of it this way: Unless they're idiots, the last thing they'll do is commit more crimes—it might hinder their escape. Since we don't have any valuables for them to steal, they wouldn't even bother with us."

"That's true," Todd reasoned. "What could they want from a bunch of kids on a camping trip?"

"Especially this hopeless bunch!" Bruce said.

"They can feel free to steal my freeze-dried lasagna!" joked Jessica, holding up her foil-sealed lunch.

"How can you joke about this?" Heather cried. "Once they find out we don't have anything of value, they'll kill us because we saw their faces. That's what happened to an entire family in Utah. Really—I saw the miniseries on TV!"

"Heather, try not to overreact," Elizabeth said gently. "This is a huge desert, and the chances of our running into the convicts are slim to absolutely none."

"Yeah, Heather, get yourself under control," Jessica said impatiently. Then she smiled, remembering a conversation she'd had with Ken one day after a tiny earthquake had shaken the school. A lot of girls were crying and carrying on to their boyfriends, and Ken had told her how annoyed he got with girls prone to histrionics.

Now she was thoroughly enjoying the fact that Heather—who was usually cool as a cucumber—was totally losing her grip.

"I can't believe you guys are just dismissing this!" Heather whined. "We're all in mortal danger!"

"Cut the dramatics, Mallone," Bruce ordered. "We're three strong guys, and they probably don't have weapons. I bet they're headed straight for Mexico, anyway."

"Bruce is right," said Elizabeth. "Let's just fuel up and try not to think about it."

Heather fretted in silence.

Jessica smiled serenely and took a nibble of her lasagna. *Not half-bad,* she realized with surprise.

"I'll give you something to think about," Bruce said, leaning forward. "One of my dad's friends, Bentley Wentworth, was camping right around here when he discovered an old mine shaft. He went in, and guess what he found?" Bruce paused dramatically.

"What?" Jessica urged.

"Tons of gold! Some guy had just abandoned it during the gold rush, and now Mr. Wentworth is loaded! We were out on his yacht a few weeks ago—he stopped by Sweet Valley on his way to Tahiti."

"Really? Wow!" Jessica exclaimed. She'd always wanted a yacht. And a Mazda Miata, and a new designer wardrobe, and a villa in Greece, and . . .

"I find that hard to believe," Elizabeth said, interrupting Jessica's daydream. "It's a lot more

61

likely that you'll be crushed to a pulp in a mine shaft than that you'll find buried treasure."

"Yeah, Bruce. That story sounds like a plot from one of Heather's soap operas," Todd agreed.

"I'm totally serious. It's true," Bruce said, raising his eyebrows and smiling enigmatically. He studied the mine entrance, which lay just a few feet from where they were sitting.

"Bruce, don't even think about it. You already have your fortune," Elizabeth said.

"But we don't, Elizabeth . . ." Jessica sighed.

"Jess, you're not serious! You actually believe Bruce?"

Jessica looked at her sister's dumbfounded face. Jessica didn't really want to go into the mine shaft—she believed Brad's warning, especially now that she saw how rotted and brittle the wooden support beams looked. But if there was a chance that a pot of gold was down there, she wasn't about to stop someone else from going in.

And why did Elizabeth constantly have to be the voice of reason? It was so predictable. Elizabeth positively thrived on telling people what they should and shouldn't do.

"Why not?" she said, standing up to pace around the area. "Wouldn't it be awesome if we found gold? Ken? Aren't you curious?"

"Count me out. I'm not risking my life for a phantom hidden treasure," Ken said, shaking his head with a dismissive wave of his hand.

"Well, I'm going in," Bruce announced suddenly.

Before anyone could comment, he grabbed a flashlight from a zippered pocket on his backpack. Without another word, he headed into the depths of the hill.

"Hey, Liz, isn't it your survival-buddy duty to follow Bruce into the mine shaft? You're supposed to stick together no matter what—or have you forgotten?" Jessica asked.

"Yeah, Elizabeth. If anything happens to him, you're responsible," Heather taunted.

Elizabeth was speechless. It wasn't her fault that Bruce was so reckless—she'd warned him not to go in. So now they expected her to put herself in danger? *Why do I always have to be the one to bear the brunt of everyone's stupidity?* she asked herself angrily. *I wish someone else would show an ounce of responsiblity, for once.*

"Don't listen to them, Liz. No one expects you to go along with Bruce on this stunt," Todd said, squeezing her hand.

"But what if the mine shaft collapses and he's trapped? Do you think you could stand it?" asked Jessica.

Elizabeth looked at her sister. Why was she pressuring Elizabeth to go into the mine shaft? But Jessica's expression didn't betray any ulterior motives.

And she was right, Elizabeth realized. Jessica knew Elizabeth wouldn't be able to live with her guilty conscience if anything did happen to Bruce. He was her buddy—they were supposed to watch out for each other.

"Jess is right. I have to find Bruce," Elizabeth finally said.

"You're not serious!" Todd exclaimed. "I can't let you do that!"

"It's not up to you, Todd. It's my job to make sure my buddy gets out of Death Valley alive. I have to face up to that."

"Have you gone completely crazy?" he asked, his voice full of dismay.

Seeing pure disbelief on Todd's face, Elizabeth wondered for a second if maybe she *had* gone a little nuts. Should she really risk her life for Bruce?

"Whether I like it or not—and I don't—I'm Bruce's buddy and I have to stick with him. Don't try to stop me, Todd."

Nobody said a word as Elizabeth retrieved her flashlight and entered the mine shaft.

Jessica watched Elizabeth descend into the darkness. As her twin's blond head disappeared, Jessica felt a sudden wave of foreboding. *Maybe I shouldn't have pressured Elizabeth about following Bruce,* she thought guiltily.

"Well, I've got my soap opera to watch," Heather announced, sitting down in front of her TV. "Ken? You coming?"

"I think I'll skip this episode, Heather. We've got enough drama right here."

Finally, thought Jessica, promptly forgetting her sense of apprehension. Now was her chance to talk to Ken about what an idiot Heather was.

Once she was sure that Heather was wrapped up in her soap, Jessica led Ken away from the others.

"Wasn't Heather being a lunatic about the fugitives? She's totally inane." Jessica laughed lightly, hoping Ken would join her.

"I guess she did get carried away," Ken said thoughtfully. "Aren't you a little scared, though?"

"Me? Scared? About something as impossible as being discovered by roaming convicts? Never! Remember, you're talking to Jessica Wakefield. I'm the Queen of Reason," she said, giving him her brightest smile while she circled her arms around his neck.

"How could I forget?" he replied, grinning.

A lock of hair stuck to Ken's forehead, giving him a rakish, sexy look. With a delicious shiver Jessica sensed a kiss was coming. She closed her eyes and felt his soft, warm lips caress her cheek, her ear, her neck. At last his lips found their way back to her mouth. Drowning in his kiss, Jessica felt all her tension melting away. Elizabeth's bossy self was safely underground, and Heather Mallone was somewhere far, far away. Unfortunately, the lovely moment didn't last long.

"Oh, Jessica," Heather's voice rang out.

"What is it?" Jessica snapped, reluctantly pulling away from Ken.

"You might want to do something about that scorpion on your ankle."

Jessica looked down in horror. A shiny brown scorpion clung to her sock, its spindly legs inching their way toward her bare leg; the creature's stingers waved threateningly. She screamed and jumped up, shaking her leg.

"Ken, help! Get it off! Get it off me!"

Ken grabbed a stick and swatted at the scorpion. It scampered away, disappearing against the brown earth.

"I got it," he said. "Did it bite you?"

Jessica willed her beating heart to stop so that she could feel whether or not she was in pain. Besides the throbbing in her brain, she didn't hurt anywhere.

"No, I guess I'm OK." Jessica didn't want Ken to think she was as silly as Heather, so she covered up her nervousness with a careless laugh. "That slimy scorpion wasn't going to have Jessica for lunch today," she said, laughing.

"Just one of the many dangers in the desert," Heather said, smiling.

Jessica wished she could find that scorpion now—and drop it down Heather's shirt. Or maybe put it in her sleeping bag. Or in her loathsome little cheerleading shoes while she slept. She could just imagine the lecture she'd get from Elizabeth.

Elizabeth! Jessica realized with a start that Elizabeth and Bruce had been gone for at least twenty minutes. Although she'd been glad to have Elizabeth out of the way for a little while, now that earlier sense of foreboding was forcing itself back into her consciousness.

"Bruce and Liz have been been in there a long time," she said out loud. "Do you think we should go in after them, Ken?"

Before Ken could answer, Heather declared, "Ken's not your buddy, Jessica. Why don't you ask your buddy to go in with you?"

Much to Jessica's annoyance, Ken didn't argue with Heather. Instead, he gave her an apologetic smile.

"You're right, Jess," Todd said. He'd gotten up from the spot where he'd been napping in the shade. "They've been in there too long for my comfort. We'd better go after them."

Jessica almost wished he'd said they shouldn't go. Looking into the mouth of the mine shaft, she wanted to see her sister's face as she never had before. The dark, dilapidated cave looked anything but welcoming.

"Come on, Jess, we'll be OK," Todd said warmly.

"Right. Let's go," Jessica answered, summoning all her courage. Just as she was about to enter the darkness, the screeching sound of Heather's voice made her cringe.

"Have fun in there, you two. Ken and I will just have to entertain ourselves while you all grope around in that dusty old mine shaft."

Jessica turned around to see Ken blushing furiously as Heather plopped down practically in his lap. *If I get out of this alive,* she swore silently, *I'm going to dedicate my life to making you miserable, Heather Mallone.*

"Come on, Todd," she said, feeling grateful that her sister had such a solid and loyal boyfriend. He would do anything for Elizabeth, Jessica realized.

Suddenly a disturbing thought entered her mind. *Would Ken risk his life to save me?* She quickly pushed the thought away—this wasn't the time to be worrying about that. *I have to focus on making sure Lizzie gets out of there alive.*

Elizabeth stopped and stood still, listening for the crunch of Bruce's feet on the ground. Silence. Bruce had forged ahead, making turn after turn. He hadn't waited for Elizabeth to catch up, and now she'd lost him.

Elizabeth waved her flashlight around the walls of the cave, trying to decide where to go next. She spotted a tunnel that looked as if it might lead back out of the mine shaft, but when she headed down it, she found herself at a dead end. She backtracked but ended up in a place that looked totally unfamiliar.

I'm lost. How am I ever going to find my way out of here? Spinning around frantically, she cursed Bruce for putting her in this horrible predicament. But blaming Bruce wasn't going to help her now. Her only hope was to keep moving, so she pushed away her growing panic and headed down yet another tunnel.

Suddenly Elizabeth tripped over something on the ground, landing on her palms with a thud. When she looked down, she saw a rusted pickax half-buried in loose dirt. She picked it up, realizing in awe that it had probably been there for over a hundred years. In her mind she conjured up an image of the men who had worked down there, searching for gold.

Then out of the corner of her eye she glimpsed a leather strap a few feet away from where she was squatting. *What's this?* she wondered. She pulled on the strap and yanked hard.

The strap was attached to a worn leather satchel. Her heart pounding with excitement, she undid the rusty buckle and opened the flap. Inside she found a canvas pouch and a bunch of yellowed papers.

Squinting her eyes in the flickering beam of the flashlight, Elizabeth examined the papers more closely. They looked like some pages torn from a diary. Deciphering the handwriting in the diary, she saw that it was dated 1849. "Right in the middle of the big California Gold Rush!" she said to herself. Elizabeth started to read one of the diary entries, a surge of adrenaline coursing through her veins.

We only have enough food and water to last us four days in the desert, but my companions insist upon entering every single mine shaft we encounter. I can't believe that out of the six of us, I am the only one voicing reason. If we do make it through this desert alive, that's good enough for me. Life itself is a treasure—who needs gold?

Elizabeth shivered as an eerie sensation washed over her. Then her mind jumped to another thought: What an amazing story! She was uncovering history—she could get published with this, for sure. She flipped to the next page.

I never would have predicted it, but it seems as though I was too quick to dismiss the promise of the desert. . . .

Elizabeth glanced up with alarm as a loud rumble broke the silence of the cave. Her eyes widened as she saw debris loosening from the walls. With a crack one of the ceiling support beams split and swung down, nearly hitting her in the back of the head. The mine shaft was collapsing! *I'm going to be buried alive if I don't get out of here now!* she thought frantically.

Without stopping to think, she gathered up the satchel and ran back in the direction she'd come, praying that she'd be able to find her way out before the earth caved in around her. The rumbles came louder and more furious. Pebbles and rocks showered down from the walls of the ancient mine shaft. Elizabeth covered her head with the satchel and stumbled on, feeling her eyes burn with a mix of sweat, dust, and tears. Blood pounded in her head as she fought to quell her rising hysteria.

Finally, in the distance, a narrow ray of light shone on the wall of the cave. With a rush of relief Elizabeth raced toward it. The roar of the collapsing earth was almost deafening. Then she stopped. Bruce! He was probably still inside—she had to get him out! A split second later the crack of another ceiling beam shattered her resolve. Praying that Bruce had the sense to escape on his own, she charged toward the light.

The first thing she saw when the dust cleared was Bruce, leaning back on his hands, idly chewing on a dried piece of grass. Elizabeth breathed a sigh of relief.

"Good going, Wakefield. I thought I was going to have to go in after you," Bruce said smugly.

For a moment a red haze of fury clouded Elizabeth's vision. She'd almost died, and Bruce was trying to act as if he hadn't even been scared!

"If you'd stuck by me like you were supposed to, I wouldn't have been nearly buried alive! That's the whole point of the buddy system!"

"Well, excuse me for living," Bruce said. He laughed harshly.

"Sometimes, Bruce Patman, I could just, I could just—" Too angry to finish her sentence, Elizabeth stormed over to her pack to get some water. *I'm not going to let him get to me. I'm not going to let him get to me,* she said to herself, the words a silent mantra. She didn't even notice that everyone else from the group was nowhere to be seen.

"What were you two lovebirds doing?" Elizabeth heard Bruce ask. She looked up to see Heather and Ken appear from behind a boulder. Ken was holding a small bouquet of wildflowers.

"Ken and I went back on the trail to pick up some of these beautiful wildflowers I'd noticed," Heather replied, beaming.

Ken looked at Elizabeth and blushed.

"This desert isn't a florist's shop, it's a complex ecosystem, Heather. You can't just desecrate nature like that!" scolded Elizabeth. But before she could go on, Ken looked at the pile of rubble that had once been the entrance to the mine shaft.

"What happened?" he cried.

"Oh, my gosh, Ken, it was awful," Elizabeth said, her recent terror rushing back. "Thanks to Bruce, we were almost buried alive!" It was then that she noticed Jessica and Todd were missing. "Where are Jess and Todd?" she asked warily.

"They went in after you! Didn't they find you?" Ken asked, obviously panic-stricken.

Elizabeth went cold. The walls had been on the brink of crashing down on top of her; she was sure the mine shaft was rubble by now. Elizabeth barely breathed as she contemplated the grim possibilities. *Jessica and Todd might have been killed—trying to save my life.*

Chapter 5

"There's still time! Start digging now, and we might find them before they suffocate!"

Elizabeth came to her senses at the sound of Ken's voice. She rushed to the pile of backpacks. *And I wondered why in the world we'd need these,* she thought as she tossed the collapsible shovels over to where Ken, Bruce, and Heather stood ready to dig.

Elizabeth said a silent prayer. *You are the two people I love most in the world. And now you may have lost your lives to save mine. Please, oh, please be alive!*

"Wait!" Bruce yelled. "I think I hear something!" Rocks and wood tumbled to the ground in front of the cave, and two bodies pushed their way through the loose pile of debris.

"It's them!" shouted Bruce.

"They're alive!" Ken shouted.

"What a relief!" sighed Heather.

"Jess! Todd! Thank goodness you're OK!" cried Elizabeth. Jessica and Todd emerged from the rubble, covered in dust and gasping for air between coughs. Elizabeth rushed to Todd.

"Hold on to me, Todd," she said, grabbing him around the waist to support him. Todd threw his arms around her shoulders as he tried to catch his breath. "Here, sit down." She guided him to a patch of dried grass, and they sank together to the ground.

Ken rushed to Jessica and embraced her. "You've never looked more beautiful to me than you do right now," he said quietly, wiping the grime from her face and hair. Jessica hugged Ken tightly, her knees buckling. They made their way to the grass and collapsed.

"You guys OK?" Bruce asked, an unmistakable note of concern in his voice.

"Yeah, are you all right?" asked Heather, who was standing awkwardly next to Bruce.

Todd coughed. "I don't seem to be injured. How 'bout you, Jess?"

Jessica took a deep breath. "I guess—" Some dust caught in her throat, and her body shook with another coughing fit. Ken stroked her back and circled his arms around her shoulders. Finally the coughs subsided. "I guess I'm OK," she breathed.

"To think that you guys almost died in there—" Heather gasped.

"Heather!" Elizabeth barked. "We're all shaken up as it is. You don't have to make things worse."

"Sorry, I wasn't thinking," Heather murmured.

74

"It's OK, Heather," Todd said gently. "I have a feeling we're all thinking the same thing."

"I'm thinking that I will be forever grateful to you and Jessica for risking your lives for us," Elizabeth said, tears in her eyes.

"Believe me," said Jessica, who had finally caught her breath, "if I had known this could happen, I never would have let you go into that mine shaft in the first place," she said.

Ignoring the fact that it was Jessica who had convinced her to follow Bruce, Elizabeth felt an overwhelming rush of love for her sister.

"Yeah, Liz—Jess was the one who said we should go in after you," Todd said.

"You did?"

"It wasn't even a question—I couldn't let fear stop me. I knew what I had to do." Jessica paused dramatically, throwing back her shoulders.

Elizabeth felt incredibly proud of her sister. *Jess really showed a lot of courage, going into that cave,* she thought. *I knew she had it in her.* She got up and went over to Jessica. They hugged warmly, holding on to each other for a long time.

Ken stood up. "Hey, pal," he said to Todd, giving him a friendly hug and a slap on the back. "It's sure great to see you. I don't know what I would have done if anything had happened to you." Elizabeth heard Ken's voice catch and noticed that his eyes were watering a little.

"Thanks, man," Todd replied, returning the hug.

"How about some water, Jess?" Bruce offered his canteen.

"Thanks, Bruce." Jessica reached for the water and took a long drink.

Here's a little bit of the human Bruce I remembered, Elizabeth thought fondly. *It just took something like this to bring it out.*

"Todd, you want some?" Jessica handed the canteen to Todd, who downed a huge swig.

"This place gives me the creeps," Heather said with a shudder. "I say we get out of here—we've got to stay ahead of the convicts."

"Are you still fixated on that?" Bruce scoffed.

"I'm the only one facing reality here. Those criminals are going to find us."

"Heather, I think it's best that we try not to worry about it," Elizabeth said. She didn't want everyone to get distracted by the minuscule possibility that they'd meet up with the convicts. They had to stay focused on reaching their destination.

In truth, the place spooked her, too. Not because she feared the impossible—that some convicts would terrorize them—but because of what had just happened. *We had a brush with death,* she reminded herself. *And it's only the second day.*

"We might as well get moving," she said out loud. "Are you guys ready to go?" She looked from Todd to Jessica.

"Most definitely." Jessica sighed, bending down to retrieve her pack.

"Let's go," Todd said.

They gathered their things in silence. Elizabeth picked up the shovels where everyone had dropped them when Jessica and Todd had appeared.

Folding the shovels into their portable sleeves, Elizabeth's eye caught a small rodent a few feet away. She watched as it burrowed into the earth until it disappeared, leaving nothing but a small pile of loose brown dirt. Seeing the animal disappear under the earth sent her mind reeling with visions of the fate she'd so narrowly escaped.

Rocks dropping everywhere, dust in her throat, Elizabeth clawed her way through the dark, dry earth, grabbing at falling beams of wood. She struggled to reach the mouth of the mine shaft. Every breath scorched her sore lungs. Without warning her foot slipped on some loose gravel, and she fell down, rocks and dirt tumbling on top of her. She saw the little speck of light above her getting smaller and smaller until it was gone. . . .

"We should have listened to Kay and Brad," she said to the group, snapping a shovel handle closed. "They knew what they were talking about when they warned us to stay away from the mine shafts. For the rest of this trek I suggest we follow the rules—they're meant to protect us." She stared meaningfully at Bruce.

"Hey, I didn't ask anyone to follow me in."

"But don't you get it, Bruce? Once you went in, I had to go with you. And Jess and Todd had to come after us. We're as responsible for your safety as you are. Just like you're responsible for ours," she said authoritatively.

"If you'd let me go in by myself, Wakefield, everything would have been fine. All of us in there together is probably what made it collapse."

"Still, one thing we know for certain is that nothing would have happened if you hadn't insisted on going in, Bruce," Ken commented.

"Yeah, Bruce," Heather accused.

"So now everyone's ganging up on me, huh? I thought we were supposed to be a team," he said sarcastically.

"A team's only as good as its members," Elizabeth snapped.

Bruce puffed out his chest, looking ready for a fight.

"Hey, everyone, there's no need to get into a big fight over this. We're all OK, so let's just put it behind us," said Todd.

For someone who almost lost his life, Todd sure is calm, Elizabeth thought, watching him wipe the thin coating of dust from his T-shirt and shorts. *I should follow his lead.*

"Todd's right." She forced herself to smile at the whole group. "This was really scary and I got upset. I'm just glad you're safe, Bruce. I'm glad we're all safe." She winked at Jessica. "On with the hike!"

"What's that?" Jessica asked, pointing at the brown leather bag lying on the ground.

"Oh, I almost forgot." She had dropped the satchel when she'd escaped the mine shaft. Her earlier fascination flooded back as she knelt to the ground and pulled the yellowed pages out of the pouch.

"I found this tucked away in the mine shaft. It has part of an old diary in it! Listen to this . . ." she said, looking up. But no one seemed to be paying attention; their eyes were riveted to the worn canvas bag that had slid out of the satchel.

"What's in there?" asked Jessica.

"I don't know, I didn't look in it." Elizabeth shrugged. Didn't anyone care that she'd made the kind of historical discovery most people just dreamed about?

"Well, let's check it out!" Bruce said, reaching to grab for it.

"OK, OK," said Elizabeth, retrieving the pouch before Bruce could snatch it up. Loosening the strings, she shook it open and poured out the contents.

Elizabeth gasped. Gold nuggets tumbled out onto the ground, glittering brightly in the sunlight.

Nobody breathed and nobody moved. Jessica couldn't believe her eyes. Bruce was right! There *was* gold in the mine shafts!

"We're rich!" Jessica cried after a long moment. "Oh, Elizabeth, you are the best sister any girl could wish for!" She rushed to gather up the nuggets that were rolling away, accidentally bumping into her sister.

"Hey, watch it!" Elizabeth shouted, losing her balance. Todd moved to catch her before she fell.

"Not so fast, Wakefield," Bruce said to Jessica. He pushed Todd aside and started collecting pieces himself. "Whose idea was it to go into the mine shaft in the first place?" he said, seizing the pouch.

"Oh, give me a break, Patman!" Jessica said, trying to push Bruce away. "Elizabeth found it—"

"Stop it, both of you!" Elizabeth interrupted

sternly. "We don't know *who* the gold belongs to. Somebody might have just stored it there."

"Be serious, Liz!" Jessica scoffed. "Who would be stupid enough to store gold in a cave?"

"And how would we know whose it is, anyway? It doesn't have anybody's name on it," Bruce challenged.

"Are you forgetting that I also found a diary? Something in these pages might tell us whose it is. If the gold doesn't belong to anyone," she said, looking from Jessica to Bruce, "then of course we'll divide it equally six ways. That's the only solution."

"But, Liz! You found it! And I risked my life to save you! The gold is ours!" Jessica cried.

"Sorry, Jess, no go," Bruce cut in. "Elizabeth found it, but only because she followed me in. I'd consider it fair if I gave her half."

"It might not even be ours to split!" Elizabeth said with exasperation.

"Give her half? But she—"

"What about us? We should get a part of it, too!" whined Heather.

"Get a grip on yourselves!" Todd's voice boomed. "I think we should listen to Elizabeth— she found the gold. And she's right. Somebody might be coming back for it."

"Thank you, Todd," Elizabeth said. "I thought everyone was going completely nuts."

Todd beamed. He was glad to be on Elizabeth's side on this one. Plus, he was happy to see the wedge between her and Bruce getting bigger and bigger.

"What else is in the bag? Maybe it'll give us a clue about whose gold this is," Todd said.

"Let's see." Elizabeth peered into the satchel. "Hmmm, what's this?" She pulled out a folded-up piece of paper. Everyone gathered around her as she unfolded it, section by section.

"What is it? What is it?" Jessica urged.

"Calm down—I don't want to tear it." Finally Elizabeth held it open.

"A treasure map!" Ken exclaimed, his eyes flashing with delight.

"This keeps getting better and better," cheered Heather, jumping up and down with excitement.

Ken and Todd each gripped a corner and held up the map. Everyone looked over their shoulders to study it. Although Todd hadn't paid much attention during the map-reading part of their lessons, he could tell that markings on this map looked remarkably similar to those on their own.

"This is where we are!" he decided.

"Of course it is, bonehead," blurted Bruce. "What did you think, it would be a map of Sweden?"

"Well, it could have been to somewhere else," Todd said defensively. Then he took a deep breath. *I can't let Bruce get to me,* he reminded himself.

"Look! What do you think those black *X*'s mean?" asked Jessica.

"If you guys would calm down for a minute, I'll read the diary and find out," Elizabeth said, flipping through the yellowed pages. "Here, I think I've found it," she said after a moment. Elizabeth read out loud: "'On the second day of our journey through the desert, we've hit the jackpot.'"

"They said 'jackpot' back then?" whispered Ken to Jessica.

"Ssshhhh—let her read," Jessica whispered back. Elizabeth continued:

"'I've heard many a traveler tell the story of the Treasure of the Scorpion, but never did I believe them until today. Now that I know the treasure is real, I know the stories I've heard about the curse are real as well.

"'This is the rule of the Treasure of the Scorpion: He who finds the gold must copy the map and split the gold in half, leaving half the gold and the map for the next lucky traveler.'"

"We're the next lucky traveler!" squealed Heather.

"Be quiet and let her read," commanded Bruce.

Elizabeth read on: "'He who does not follow the rule of the Treasure of the Scorpion will be cursed.'"

Elizabeth stopped short. No one spoke.

"That's it?" exclaimed Jessica. "What's the curse? What happens to you?"

"I don't know, it doesn't say," Elizabeth said, turning over the page.

"I guess this means the gold doesn't belong to anyone else, right, Liz?" Jessica declared with a huge smile, her eyes glistening.

"Yay! We found gold!" Heather yelled.

"So this is half of what the last person found back in 1849!" Ken said.

"That's right!" shouted Bruce. "That means, chances are, whoever left this gold here left more gold at these other sites. . . ." He pointed to the other *X*'s that dotted the map.

For once Todd felt as if he and Bruce were on the same wavelength; there was more treasure to be found. Todd could have sworn he felt his mouth water.

"So you want us to abandon our course and go in search of this treasure?" Elizabeth asked. She looked from one face to the next. Bruce's enthusiasm was obvious as he pored over the treasure map. Jessica's eyes had glassed over; her impish grin told Elizabeth she was already spending the gold in her imagination. Heather had her eyes on Ken and seemed to be waiting to hear his opinion. Todd and Ken were the only ones in the group who looked as if they were inwardly wrestling over the decision.

"Well," Ken started, "we do have strict instructions, and we weren't even supposed to have entered the mine shaft in the first place. How's it going to look when we come back with the gold we've already found?"

"But we were told to free our minds of the expectations placed on us," Todd said earnestly. "Doesn't that include the expectations of Kay and Brad?"

"Who cares? I, for one, don't give a darn what Brad and Kay think," said Bruce.

"I hate to hear what old Chrome Dome will say when his school leaders come back with gold that they weren't even supposed to have found," Ken remarked. Chrome Dome was what all the kids called the balding principal of Sweet Valley High. "Maybe we should stick straight to the rules from here on in."

Ken had a point. Elizabeth didn't look forward to her parents' reaction when they heard how she and Jessica had nearly lost their lives over some gold. If they went after more of the treasure, Elizabeth doubted that even Jessica's extraordinary powers of justification would explain that.

"But part of the survival experience is to learn how to assess risk," continued Todd. "Yes, it was dangerous to enter the mine shaft—but sometimes risk can pay off."

"I don't even know why you guys are discussing this," Jessica interrupted. "It's ridiculous to let some stupid rules get in the way of opportunity."

Elizabeth's attention wandered from the argument. She had a debate going on in her own head. While one part of her knew that they shouldn't stray from the rules, the other part of her wanted to head straight for the black X's. *It's not the treasure I'm after, it's the incredible story!* she told herself. She was already writing the narrative in her mind.

We only had enough food and water for four days. On top of that, a tremendous storm was brewing somewhere in the heavens. But we marched on in search of treasure, uncovering the story of our ancestors who settled out west years and years ago.

She could get published with this, probably in a national magazine. Book contracts would flow in. Movie offers would follow—she could even write the screenplay. She'd be famous!

"What do you think we should do, Liz?" Ken asked, interrupting her daydream. Elizabeth came back to the present with a start. When she opened her mouth, no words came out. Her brain told her that they should stick to their course. But somehow she couldn't bring herself to say so.

"Yeah, Liz, what do you think?" Todd asked when Elizabeth didn't answer right away.

"We can guess what Miss Play-by-the-Rules Wakefield is going to say," Jessica jeered. "Out with it, Sis—I'd really like to hear your argument for passing up the chance to go after the gold. Gold that's just sitting there, waiting for someone to grab it." Jessica stood with her arms crossed in front of her, glaring at her sister.

"I'm not sure," said Elizabeth tentatively.

"Do you think we have enough time to go after more treasure and keep up with our route?" Todd asked.

"Well, actually, this X here doesn't really seem to be that far off course," Elizabeth said, referring to the map in Bruce's hands.

Jessica's eyes widened in shock. *Is sensible Elizabeth getting greedy?*

"So Elizabeth Wakefield is more interested in money than she lets on," sneered Bruce.

"It's not the gold I'm thinking about, Bruce," Elizabeth said quickly. "For a writer this could be an invaluable experience. What a great story! The other hiding places are sure to have more diary entries. Just imagine what we could learn about the lives of the gold prospectors."

Jessica rolled her eyes. "Yeah, and you're not thinking about the new computer you could buy with all that cash?"

"Well, now that you mention it, a new computer couldn't hurt my career," Elizabeth conceded. "Anyway, it looks like we can make it to tonight's camp easily before nightfall, even if we take this one detour."

"I say we go for it," Heather said. "Only an idiot would pass up such an easy chance to get rich."

Finally, something Heather and I agree on, thought Jessica. She wouldn't even consider not going for more of the gold treasure. Jessica was tired of watching her best friend, Lila Fowler, buy one expensive new outfit after another, while she had to settle for whatever happened to show up on the sales rack.

Now Jessica imagined being as rich as Lila— no, richer! She could have the best designer clothes, any car—or cars, for that matter—she wanted. She would eat only in the best restaurants, have her hair done at the most exclusive beauty salons in Beverly Hills, and vacation at high-class spas around the world. *I would live in the style I was born to enjoy,* she fantasized. *Life would be perfect.*

Jessica snapped back to the present to see everyone huddled over the two maps—the brand-new one supplied by SVSS, and the treasure map that was drawn years ago. Heather's forehead was nearly touching Ken's. *Life would be perfect, that is, if I could buy Heather's one-way ticket out of Sweet Valley,* she mentally amended.

"Do you think you can use this old map to figure out where the next treasure is, Ken?" Heather asked, looking at him with wide eyes.

"Sure, it's really pretty clear. The land hasn't changed much, even though it's been almost a hundred fifty years."

"But what do these markings mean?" she asked, touching a finger to the yellowed paper.

"That's called dirt, Heather," Bruce ridiculed.

"Don't worry about navigation," Ken said, laughing. "I can see it's not your specialty."

Heather just giggled, infuriating Jessica. Acting like a ditz was turning out to be Heather's specialty. *I can't believe Ken doesn't see right through her nauseating little dumb act,* she thought. She decided she'd better have another talk with Ken, and soon.

"I guess it's decided, then, isn't it? We're going to find the next treasure," Elizabeth said breathlessly.

"This is so cool," said Todd. He gave Elizabeth a quick hug.

"Cool? This is better than cool—it's outrageous!" Jessica cried. She forced Heather out of her mind and concentrated on something much more pleasant: She was rich! "I can't wait to tell everyone how sensational this trek has turned out to be!"

"That's for sure," Ken agreed. "I never imagined anything like this would happen to someone I knew, let alone to me!"

"Just remember who we can all thank for this—me!" said Bruce. Ken gave him a triumphant high five.

"But we've got to remember the rule of the Treasure of the Scorpion," Elizabeth warned. "We have to leave half of the treasure, and a copy of the map."

"You're right, Liz. You start copying the map, and I'll dig a hole here to leave the gold in," Todd suggested.

"Sounds good."

Jessica watched as Todd unfolded a shovel and Elizabeth dug around in her pack for some paper. *Here's the happy, loving couple, being their nerdy selves once again,* Jessica thought. Did they always have to be so conscientious? Glancing over at Bruce, she wasn't surprised to see a look of annoyed disbelief on his face.

"This gold's been here over a hundred years," Bruce argued. "Anyone who made up that asinine rule is long dead. We'd be complete chumps if we left half the gold in the ground."

Jessica jumped in immediately to support him. "Bruce is right on this one, you guys. No one here believes there really is a curse—do you?"

"It may sound crazy, but I have a gut feeling we shouldn't be breaking this rule," Elizabeth insisted, looking to Todd for support.

"I'm with Liz on this," he said.

Of course you are. When was the last time you thought for yourself? Jessica fumed silently.

"Now, this is just plain stupid," Heather said. "We're not talking about medals of honor here; this is real gold!"

"That's why I don't want to take any risks," Elizabeth said firmly.

"Actually, Liz, I'm surprised, too," said Ken. "You're so rational, I thought you'd be the last one to believe in curses."

"It's not that I believe in curses—"

"Then what? If you don't believe in curses, what possible reason could you have for wanting to leave all that gold buried in the ground?" demanded Bruce.

Jessica could tell her sister was stumped. Bruce was so clearly in the right, even master debater Elizabeth Wakefield couldn't come up with a good argument against him.

"I guess it does seem a little silly," Elizabeth allowed. "What do you think, Todd?"

"Well, I don't know. It does seem pointless, doesn't it?" he asked tentatively.

"Yeah . . . I guess it does," she conceded.

"If you don't think we have to follow the rule, I'm not going to insist," said Todd.

"OK! Six ways, right?" prompted Heather.

"Right," agreed Elizabeth.

"Let's pack up and move!" Bruce commanded.

Counting and sizing up the nuggets, they divided them into six equal piles. Jessica retrieved her gold, loving how solid it felt in her hands.

89

Where could she pack it away safely? She didn't really think any of them—not even Heather—would have the gall to steal her portion. But there was no reason to create a temptation.

Jessica sat down beside her backpack, carefully placing her treasure in her lap. She pulled out her toiletries and emptied a plastic bag containing facial cleansers. Then she dropped them in with her moisturizers. Slowly, she scooped up the gold, again savoring the feel of the cool metal as the nuggets rolled off her fingers into the bag. Sealing it tight, she glanced up to make sure no one saw exactly where she was packing her share of the treasure.

"Everybody ready?" Ken asked after a moment.

"Yup!" Jessica cheered, along with everyone else.

"Let's go," Ken called, leading the way to the next hidden treasure. The path wound up the side of a canyon dotted with sagebrush.

Walking along a narrow ridge, Jessica made the mistake of peering over the side. Her stomach turned when she saw the long drop. She had to distract herself from the thought of falling off the side and getting crushed on the rocks below. *Might as well make conversation with drone-head.*

"What're you going to do with your gold, Todd?" she inquired.

"Well, I really need a good car—I'd like to buy a brand-new one, right off the floor, paid in cash," he answered. "Then I'll probably put the rest in savings, or maybe invest some of it."

Typical, Jessica thought with a smile.

She called ahead to Ken. "What about you, Ken? What will you spend your fortune on, besides buying lots of expensive presents for me?"

Ken laughed. "If you don't clean me out first, I think I'd like a new car, too—maybe a bright-red sports car."

"Ooooh! We'll have so much fun taking drives up the coast on weekends! We could caravan—me in my beautiful Mazda Miata and you in your sports car," said Jessica, laughing.

"It's foolish to spend cash on a car," Heather said haughtily. "My mom has a friend in New York who is this totally talented jewelry designer for Diamonds International, but she needs some capital to go out on her own. I'd love to back her."

"How about you, Liz? After you buy your computer and stuff, what'll you do with the rest?" asked Todd.

"I'm thinking of investing in some art—maybe by an up-and-coming young artist. That's something I can enjoy today, and it will appreciate in value."

"Forget art," Bruce scoffed. "I'm throwing all my cash at my dad's broker. Securities are where it's at."

"Maybe we could talk about investment opportunities in the market sometime, Bruce. I've always wanted to build a portfolio," said Ken.

"I guess I could share some of my financial acumen with you, Matthews. We'll talk commission later," he said, laughing.

"I'll have my people call your people," Ken responded.

Jessica smiled. Everyone seemed to be jubilant. Jessica looked out over the valley. The distant mountain peaks had turned from gray to red as the afternoon sun moved in the sky. Her steps confident, she had an overall feeling of well-being. She was rich, and she was going to get even richer. At the moment she didn't even feel the animosity toward Heather that had been weighing her down. *This trip is turning out to be one of the best things I've ever done*, she told herself. *Who knew?*

Chapter 6

"Use that root as a handhold," Todd called down to Jessica from the top of a boulder. "Here, let me help you," he said, offering his hand.

"No, it's OK, I got it," Jessica responded, grasping the root and pulling herself up with a grunt.

Todd watched as Jessica scoped the smooth face of the boulder for hand and footholds, methodically reaching, stepping, and hoisting herself up. Her eyes burned with determination and concentration, and she managed to hold her balance steady, even with the extra twenty pounds on her back.

"No prob!" She grinned triumphantly when she planted her feet firmly on top of the boulder. She wiped some sweat off her forehead with her hand, leaving a dusty smudge just above her eyes.

"You took that boulder like an expert rock climber, Jess," Todd observed, truly impressed. "Where'd you learn how to do that?"

"I'm just a natural-born athlete," Jessica said, comically flexing her arm muscles. "Where's the next one?" she asked, wiping her hands on her khaki shorts.

Todd watched her charge ahead through the obstacle course of underbrush to catch up with Ken and Heather. From the back, Jessica was a big red bouncing backpack, with sharply defined leg muscles powering her energetic steps. *Usually Jess drives me crazy—I forget that she's even related to Liz,* Todd was thinking. *But they do share some very attractive qualities.*

Todd looked down. Elizabeth, who had just reached the base of the boulder, was staring at the wall of rock. Biting her lower lip, she blew a strand of hair out of her face. Then she pulled her water bottle from her belt and gulped thirstily.

"Want me to give you some tips on getting up here?" Todd called down to her.

"Well—" said Elizabeth, eyeing the boulder with barely concealed dread.

"It's OK, Wilkins," interrupted Bruce, who had just caught up with Elizabeth. "I'll help my buddy up this one."

Elizabeth looked up at Todd, then at Bruce.

"Thanks anyway, Todd," she said, looking back up at him. "You go on and give Jessica a hand if she needs it."

Todd watched as Bruce demonstrated the proper stance and posture for rock climbing.

"Remember to keep your center of gravity real low, just above your hips," he said, bending his knees

94

slightly. "And keep your movements fluid—no sudden moves or jerks. Go ahead and start up. I'll be right behind you."

Bruce winked up at Todd as Elizabeth started climbing. *I can't let him get to me. I can't let him get to me,* Todd told himself over and over. Just because Elizabeth was accepting Bruce's help didn't mean she was going to fall for him. Did it?

"Are you sure we're still on course?" Elizabeth called to Ken, who was leading the group. "On the map it looked like the trail was relatively flat—ouch!" She stubbed her toe on a rock but caught herself before she stumbled to the ground.

"Yeah, I'm pretty sure," he shouted back. He pulled the compass out of his pocket and unfolded the treasure map again. "I don't think this old map is totally on target about the topography. We're definitely headed in the right direction."

"Just checking," Elizabeth said. "I'm sure you're right."

"It really gets your goat that you're not in charge, doesn't it, Wakefield?" gibed Bruce.

"No, Bruce, it doesn't. I was just surprised that the terrain is getting so steep."

"You getting tired, Liz?" Todd asked with concern.

"Oh, no. Not at all." Elizabeth didn't want anyone to know how sore her legs were getting. As soon as the trail flattened, she was sure her energy would pick up. Only the night before, she had congratulated herself for being in such good shape.

95

But the trail didn't flatten out. Just when Elizabeth thought they'd reached a plateau, the ground rose again. *Can this be right? Does Ken really know what he's doing?* she wondered. Immediately Elizabeth felt ashamed of herself for the thought. Ken was a smart guy, and very conscientious. Besides her, he was probably the most responsible member of the group. She could trust him to lead the way.

She felt the burn in her thighs as the rocky trail wound its way up a steep incline. She willed herself to forget about the pain in her legs, but she couldn't ignore the ache in her back. Shifting her pack, she realized that she hadn't even thought about the weight the gold would add to their burdens.

The sun was beating down a lot stronger than it had the day before. It felt like a blowtorch was pointed straight at her brain. *I didn't think it was supposed to be so hot this time of the year,* she thought miserably. *This place must be like an oven in the summer.* Wiping her forehead with the back of her hand, Elizabeth caught a drop of sweat just before it dripped into her eyes.

"Did someone turn up the furnace?" Todd complained.

"Tell me about it—I'm roasting like a chicken on a rotisserie," Jessica said.

"More like a pig on a spit," sneered Bruce. "Want me to stuff an apple in your mouth?"

"Bruce—you just shut up," quipped Jessica.

The heat's even getting to Jess—usually she has

a snappy comeback for Bruce's teasing, Elizabeth thought.

"Why don't we stop a minute for a water break?" Elizabeth suggested.

"Great idea," Ken agreed heartily. They interrupted their climb and pulled out their canteens.

"Careful not to drink too much. A lot of water in your stomach will give you cramps," warned Elizabeth, hearing Kay's voice.

"We have to drink, Liz," Todd said. "We're sweating like crazy out here."

"I know, I know," Elizabeth conceded. "Forget it." She took a small sip of her water, savoring the wetness in her mouth before she swallowed. "Ready to hit it?"

They all took one last swig and continued their trek.

Marching up the trail, Elizabeth wasn't just thinking about her sore muscles, she was concerned about their water supply. They were still drinking the water they'd got back at the gas station. It was supposed to have got them through only two days—they'd originally figured another water supply into today's route.

Elizabeth realized with shame that in all the excitement about the gold, she'd totally forgotten that their detour wouldn't take them by a water source. But there was no way she could turn them back. It was too late.

All of a sudden Elizabeth was overcome with foreboding. *What if this heat is punishment for not leaving half the treasure behind?* She thought of the curse, and how they'd clearly disobeyed the rules of the Treasure of the Scorpion. It was obvious that the last people who'd struck it rich had yielded to the curse. Had *their* travels been as hampered by heat and exhaustion?

Then Elizabeth remembered the last time she'd let herself believe in superstitions. During a summer internship at the *London Daily News,* Elizabeth had met Luke, a young, soulful Briton who'd introduced her to werewolf lore. Just when her cynicism had started to fade, she'd found out that Luke was a psycho who thought *he* was a werewolf!

Never again will I lose grip on reality and believe in fairy tales, Elizabeth reminded herself now. *Jessica's the one who buys into silly things like superstitions and horoscopes.* She pushed any thoughts of curses out of her mind. Even so, she felt guilty about taking all of the gold. She didn't like to think of herself as greedy.

But it wasn't the gold she was after, she reminded herself. Of course she wasn't about to turn down her own fortune; but what was really driving her was her soon-to-be-blossoming career. She could certainly get a story published in *Outdoor Adventure* magazine. Or maybe in *World Traveler,* which catered to the travel connoisseur. The diaries she'd found would probably shed some light on the history of the California Gold Rush. She pictured herself traveling the academic circuit, giving talks at universities and research institutes. Maybe a museum would feature her discoveries in an exhibit.

This was such an amazing opportunity, how could she possibly think anything bad could come of it? And by this time tomorrow they'd be right back on course; they could get water then. After all, just one day of not getting quite enough to drink wouldn't hurt anyone, would it?

"We'll definitely reach water tomorrow," Elizabeth said out loud to Bruce. "We can just be sure to compensate for the fluids we're not getting today."

"Yeah, sure," said Bruce, who didn't sound at all concerned.

Feeling much better, Elizabeth took stock of the rest of the group. Despite the wicked heat, spirits seemed high. She saw that Jessica and Todd were engaged in a lively conversation, but she couldn't hear what they were talking about. *I could be the one having fun with Todd, instead of trudging along in silence with Bruce,* she realized with a pang of regret. Then she pushed the thought away. She'd always wished that Jessica and Todd would bury their differences and learn to like each other. *I'm happy that they have this opportunity to hang out together,* she reminded herself.

Elizabeth decided to turn her attention to Bruce. Now that they'd found the treasure, maybe Bruce would be easier to talk to. She couldn't be the only one who didn't like to hike in this tense silence. If she could just tap into his interests . . . *Hmmm, what does Bruce love more than anything? Money!* She thought back to the guest speaker who had come to her social-studies class to talk about the stock market.

"Bruce, what kind of stocks do you think you'll use your gold to invest in?" she asked.

Bruce turned around and eyed Elizabeth, looking suspicious. He raised his eyebrows and shrugged. "Well, since you ask, my dad's been talking a lot about health-care companies," he said flatly.

He didn't seem to believe that she wanted to talk about investments, so she said with enthusiasm, "Oh, yeah? Why's that?"

Bruce turned around and looked at Elizabeth again. "That's a service industry that has nowhere to go but up, what with all the aging baby boomers." Now he was getting animated.

"You're right, that does sound promising," Elizabeth commented.

Bruce continued. "But I don't know—I might put some of it in a low-risk mutual fund to be safe and use the rest in a higher-risk investment. I've been reading all about the commodities market. Futures can pay off big time. Or they can soak you." He turned around to see if she was still paying attention.

Bruce looks really attractive when he's into what he's doing. She thought of his intensity when he played tennis. It was always impossible not to notice how sexy Bruce looked when he was in the middle of a close match.

"My dad said when he was starting out, he took a big hit on the commodities exchange," Elizabeth said, feeling proud that she even knew what Bruce was talking about.

"Yeah, that can happen. It's not a place for beginners," Bruce said with authority.

Elizabeth smiled to herself, wondering how much experience Bruce actually had.

As they continued chatting about the market and investments, Elizabeth realized that this was the most they'd talked since their short romance. The wall that had grown between them seemed to be breaking down, and she was glad. Elizabeth decided to tell him about her plans to publish the story of their adventure.

"Cool," he said with enthusiasm after she'd described her ambitions. "Just as long as you make me the hero—after all, if it weren't for me, we wouldn't have struck gold," he said with a laugh.

Elizabeth laughed, too. *When he isn't taking himself so seriously, Bruce can be a really cool guy,* she observed. For the first time in months she remembered why she used to find Bruce so attractive. And now that she remembered, Elizabeth had a feeling it might not be so easy to forget again soon.

"These straps are killing me!" Heather whined, tugging at her backpack. "My pack feels twice as heavy as it felt this morning. I never knew gold was this heavy."

"That's because you're only used to the cheap gold-plated trinkets you call jewelry," Jessica said. Heather stopped in her tracks and looked down the trail.

"I'll have you know, Wakefield, that I only wear pure metals," she retorted. "Actually, my mother's friend at Diamonds International says that all the best brides this year are getting platinum settings. Platinum is my favorite—gold is so pedestrian."

"If this gold isn't good enough for you, Ms. Mallone, I'll be happy to ease your load," offered Bruce sarcastically, fingering the buckles on her pack.

"Oh, no, you don't, Patman." Heather squirmed away from Bruce. "This stuff isn't for wearing, it's for spending!"

"Maybe it's time for another water break," Elizabeth broke in.

Jessica looked at her sister in surprise. For someone who was usually so upbeat and gung ho, Elizabeth sounded uncharacteristically tired and grumpy.

"Good idea, Elizabeth. I think we're all pretty beat," Ken said.

At that Heather sank immediately to the ground. "Oh, Ken, I'm so tired!" she wailed.

Jessica was taken aback. Heather usually acted as if nothing could faze her. *If Heather's going to pull off the frail act, on top of the stupid act she's been playing, I'm going to show Ken just how resilient I am,* she decided. If there was one thing Jessica couldn't stand, it was girls who played weak and dumb because they thought it was attractive to guys. *Heather and her kind are a disgrace to the gender.* She pulled back her drooping shoulders and stood up straight.

"Gee, Heather, I thought you were in better shape," Jessica said. "Elizabeth and I aren't tired, are we, Liz?"

"I'm OK," Elizabeth responded, not sounding very sincere. "Just parched with thirst." She took a gulp of water.

"Well, the sun's getting lower on the horizon—shall we move on before it starts getting dark?" Ken asked the group after a couple of minutes.

"I'm ready!" Jessica said perkily.

"Heather?" Ken held out a hand to help Heather to her feet. For someone who complained about being so tired, she stood up pretty smoothly, Jessica noticed.

"Thanks, Ken," Heather said sweetly. Jessica felt nauseous.

"Let's go!" Ken urged.

The trail had leveled off by now, so they progressed a little faster. But their path was hindered by clumps of nasty-looking gray bushes with especially voracious thorns; although Jessica tried to avoid getting scraped, her shins kept getting poked and pierced.

Stepping around one bush, Jessica was jarred by the sight of an empty cigarette pack stuck into its side. It looked completely out of place. She should probably pick it up; she didn't like seeing litter. But the bush would practically attack her if she reached inside it, she realized. *Forget it—I'm not the one who littered, anyway.*

The mountain peaks in the distance turned from red to orange to periwinkle as the sun fell lower in the sky. But Jessica couldn't enjoy the beauty of the sunset. She was too worried that they wouldn't make it to the next treasure while it was still light.

"My feet hurt," Heather whined suddenly, slowing down. "And it's getting dark. Ken, are you sure you know what you're doing? Will you be able to navigate in the dark?"

"It shouldn't be a problem," Ken said. "I have the compass, so I don't need the sun to know what direction we're going in. That's the most important thing."

Even though he spoke with self-assurance, Jessica detected a slight note of worry in his voice. Her heart filled with love. *He's so cute when he's anxious*, she thought.

"I've seen you pull some tremendous plays on the football field, Ken," she said aloud. "I know you can do this."

"Thanks for the vote of confidence, Jess," Ken said, looking at Jessica gratefully.

She noticed with glee that Heather was bristling. *Support and loyalty through thick and thin is what true love is all about—something you'll never understand, Heather Mallone.*

When the sun finally disappeared, and the sky deepened from azure-blue to navy, Jessica was surprised by how much the moon's glow illuminated the barren terrain. Still, it wasn't enough to hike by, so they all pulled out flashlights to find their way. Gusts of wind picked up dust and dry leaves, bringing a chill to the air. Jessica pulled out a sweatshirt to ward off the cold.

At the base of a tall, narrow peak, Ken stopped. "I think we've made it," he announced, shining his flashlight at the map and the compass.

"Thank God," Heather sighed. They all gathered around the map.

"See?" Ken pointed out their location. "This peak here looks like the one they drew on the map."

"Good job, Ken." Todd slapped his friend on the back.

"No one doubted you, Ken," said Elizabeth supportively.

Heather planted a big kiss on Ken's cheek. "I knew you could do it," she said sweetly.

"Give me a—" Jessica started with undisguised disgust.

"It's OK, you guys, I was a little nervous myself," Ken admitted.

"Enough with all this backslapping," Bruce said excitedly. "There's gold hidden somewhere around here."

"Yeah, let's get the search going," Jessica said, dropping her pack to the ground with a thump. They spread themselves over the area, each determined to find what they were looking for.

"I don't even know what to look for," Heather said, wandering aimlessly, kicking up dust.

"Look for something that could be a hiding place, Einstein," snorted Jessica as she crawled around under a bush.

"Like you're a genius yourself," retorted Heather. "When's the last time you used your brain?"

Jessica stood up and glared at Heather across the bush. Heather glared back.

Will these two just put a lid on it already? thought Bruce as he explored a rock wall for some sort of hole. Their constant bickering was getting really tedious.

Then he spotted the mouth of a cave. This was it! He shone his flashlight and saw the beam of light disappear into the depths of the cave. "Hey, guys! Look what I found! I bet they hid the gold down here," he shouted to the others.

Jessica reached him first. "What are we waiting for?" she cried. "Let's go in!"

"My sentiments exactly." The anticipation of putting his hands on another bag of gold was making Bruce's heart race and his blood pound.

"Maybe we should wait until morning, when it's light," Elizabeth suggested.

"Talk about Einstein—it'll be dark inside the cave no matter what!" Heather laughed. She nudged Ken and rolled her eyes.

"Come on, Liz." Todd gently brushed Elizabeth's hair away from her face. "Could you really go to sleep without knowing what's in this cave?" he asked.

"I guess you're right," Elizabeth said, peering inside the cave.

Watching Elizabeth's eyes light up with excitement, Bruce thought back to the way she'd gotten so animated when she'd talked about getting published. He liked the fact that Elizabeth had such strong ambitions. She was different from most girls her age—she had determination, stamina, and talent. *That's what I liked about her before, and that's what I still like about her,* he realized. *Maybe I should take advantage of this buddy system. . . .*

"Liz and I can go first!" he said with renewed purpose.

"Uhh, Bruce? Remember the last time you went rushing into the earth, and we all almost died?" Jessica said with a smirk.

Bruce winced. It was typical of Jessica to touch a sore spot—but he had no intention of showing the others that he felt guilty about that mine shaft collapsing.

"Fine, Wakefield. If you guys are nervous about something happening, why don't we tie a rope between each other so we're all attached?"

"That's a good idea, Bruce," Elizabeth said. With Bruce and Elizabeth in front and Jessica and Todd bringing up the rear, they all looped the rope around their waists, keeping about five feet of distance between each other.

Nobody spoke as they crept slowly into the cave. Bruce stepped carefully; the ground was slippery and the cave walls shone with moisture. What if there was one of those underground streams there? He suddenly had the image of water rushing through the cave at them. *Don't be ridiculous, Patman, we're in the desert—there can't be that much water.*

He concentrated on finding the treasure, scouring the wet rocky walls for a suitable hiding place. He wanted to be the one to discover the gold this time.

"This totally looks like a place where convicts

would be hiding out," Heather said fearfully, pulling the group to a halt.

"Heather, we're all tied together now, so you're just going to have to keep moving," Bruce commanded. Heather was turning out to be such a paranoid, sniveling whiner.

"I'm moving, I'm moving," she said defensively.

"Don't worry—I'm positive we're the only human life in this cave," Ken said consolingly.

That's for sure, thought Bruce. *I don't know what kind of idiot would hang out in this creepy place.* Then he heard a strange flapping noise. "What the—" He broke off as the noise got closer and closer. *What is that?* Suddenly it was on top of him, and something brushed his forehead. Bats!

"Watch your heads!" he yelled out, ducking.

Everyone screamed and fell to the ground as a flock of bats circled and dived over their heads. Then, as quickly as the bats had appeared, they were gone.

"Yuck!" Jessica yelled, brushing off her shorts.

"I've never run into bats before," Todd said, looking to see where they'd flown.

"OK, everyone, they're gone," said Bruce, urging the group onward. And onward. How deep was this cave? After a few more minutes he reached a fork. One corridor veered uphill, while the other seemed to lead deeper into the earth.

"Which way should we go?" Elizabeth asked.

"I don't know." Bruce shone his flashlight into each of the paths.

"Maybe we should split up," suggested Todd.

"Good idea," Bruce said. He wouldn't mind being alone with Elizabeth—especially in the dark. "I'll go with Liz up here—you guys go down that way."

"Umm, OK," Elizabeth said tentatively, looking back at Todd.

"Be careful, you guys," Todd called, after Bruce and Elizabeth had separated themselves from the rest of the group and started up the corridor.

"We'll be fine," Bruce called back, taking Elizabeth's hand. Her fingers felt soft and cool in his palm. He gripped her tighter, pulling her close. "Be careful not to slip," he said gently.

"I'm OK," she said, returning his grip.

Now separated from the others, in this dark, intimate place, Bruce could hold it in no longer. He had to ask her—did she feel that strange, latent attraction between them pushing its way to the surface?

"Liz?" he started, turning around to face her.

"What is it?" she asked. Her lips were inches away from his. Bruce remembered exactly what it felt like to kiss them. He wanted to kiss them now.

"Stop! I think I found it!" Jessica's voice echoed through the tunnels.

Looking startled, Elizabeth backed away from Bruce. *Darnit!* Bruce cursed. *Jessica Wakefield is always cramping my style.*

"We'd better find them," Elizabeth said, sounding a little out of breath. "What were you going to say?"

"Nothing," mumbled Bruce. "Let's go."

Leaving the cave, they moved a lot faster. Elizabeth breathed a sigh of relief when she and Bruce emerged from the cave. She didn't want to think about what had almost happened between them.

"Check it out! This one has four bags of gold!" Jessica cried, unpacking four canvas pouches.

The wind had picked up while they'd been underground, and Elizabeth tried to ignore the cold that seeped into her bones.

"Let's look at the gold!" Heather said with excitement. They huddled on the ground and shone their flashlights into the circle, examining the contents of the pouches. Watching the others, Elizabeth was sickened. *They look like vultures*, she thought.

But when Todd handed her a sack, she felt her breath catch in her throat. Her palms got sweaty and her fingers tingled when she saw the size of the glittering nuggets. *I'm just as bad as they are*, Elizabeth realized with a start. *It's really sick what a little gold can do to a person.*

She reminded herself of what she should *really* be excited about: the diary. "Well, we've determined that there's a lot of treasure here, so let's see what else we've found," she said out loud.

"Here's the diary, and another map," Todd said, handing the yellowed papers straight to Elizabeth. She flipped through the diary entries as the others continued to ogle the gold.

"Listen to this," she said. "'We've made it to the

second hiding place and were surprised to discover a huge stash. The others tried to convince me that we could probably get away with leaving less than half the gold, that we wouldn't be cursed. But when I reminded them of the story of Old Johnny Lock, they stopped their foolishness.'"

Elizabeth looked around at the others, but no one met her eye. Not even Todd—he was absorbed in the map and didn't appear to be listening.

"From the looks of this map, there should be one final treasure," he announced. "See these three X's?"

Elizabeth's eyes widened. *More treasure?* She scanned the diary entries until she found what she was looking for.

"Listen to this, everybody." She cleared her throat and picked up reading where she'd left off: "'After much discussion, we've agreed to risk it and search for the last treasure. The payoff is too great to ignore.'"

"What else does it say? What were their risks?" Ken asked anxiously.

"I don't know." Elizabeth squinted her eyes and tried to read through the rest of the tattered papers.

"But they went for it!" cried Jessica, her eyes shining bright. "We've got to go for it, too."

"No doubt!" Bruce agreed breathlessly. He seemed completely mesmerized by the bag of gold in his hand.

"Only if we could make it there and still be on schedule," Elizabeth said. "Give me a minute to figure out how long it would take us." She stood up to get a pen and paper from her pack.

"Don't be such a worrywart, Liz. How far could it be?" Jessica stared at Elizabeth, a look of irritation on her face. "Some opportunities are just too good to pass up."

Elizabeth opened her mouth to respond, but Ken cut in.

"I think your sister has a point, Jess. We're a little off schedule already, and we only have two more days before we have to be at Desert Oasis."

"Thank you, Ken," Elizabeth said. "It's not like I don't want to go after the gold, but we need to know if we can make it." In spite of herself, Elizabeth was hoping they'd have time to go after the next treasure. The vision of gold nuggets sparkled in her brain as she did some quick calculations with the map and compass.

Her heart sank. If they took another detour to the last spot on the map, they wouldn't be able to make it to Desert Oasis in time to meet the bus and avoid the storm.

"Schedule, schmedule," scoffed Jessica when Elizabeth announced her conclusion.

"This isn't just about staying on schedule, Jessica. This is about survival," Elizabeth chastised.

"It doesn't look that far to me. We could pick up the pace and stop taking breaks all the time," Bruce offered, casting a glare at Heather.

"I'm willing to sacrifice watching my show for the good of the group," she said haughtily.

"I'm telling you, there's no way we can make

it." Elizabeth glared at Bruce defiantly.

"You just want to make all the decisions, Wakefield. And to think I was actually beginning to like you again."

So he *was* feeling the old attraction again, Elizabeth realized with a start. What would she have done if he'd tried to kiss her in the cave? Would she have kissed him back? She shook her head. *If there was something going on between us, it's over now. Bruce is still a pigheaded jerk.*

"I don't know about the rest of you, but I'd like to reach our pickup point before the storm hits," she said, staring Bruce down. It was a challenge of wills—Elizabeth's and Bruce's. She caught Todd looking at her suspiciously.

"Chill out on the lecture, Liz," Bruce said after a few moments.

"Yeah—who says you get to decide for us all? I'm with Bruce." Jessica gave Bruce a wide smile.

"It's not who's right or who's wrong. We've got to face reality: We're not going to make it."

"How do we know you didn't figure wrong?" Bruce asked, narrowing his eyes.

"I didn't figure wrong, Bruce. I even accounted for us moving faster." Elizabeth returned his gaze.

"I never knew you were so power hungry," Jessica said loudly.

"It's not about power or being in charge, Jess!" Elizabeth swung to face her sister. Why did everything turn into a battle? Didn't Bruce and Jessica see that they were all on the same side? "I'm not a dictator here—we can all make

113

the decision together. Todd? Ken? What do you guys think?"

"You're sure we can't make it?" asked Todd with obvious disappointment.

"Even if we walk faster and longer each day?" Ken prompted.

"Absolutely sure. It's not like I don't want to go for the treasure, too, you guys. It's just too risky." She saw that Ken and Todd were slowly coming to her side. "Remember how we thought we'd make it here well before dark?"

"That's true. I guess you're right," Todd conceded. "We'd better forget about the rest."

"Don't look so glum, Wilkins," said Ken. "Look at what we've got sitting right in front of us. And that's on top of what we've been carrying around all afternoon."

Elizabeth looked over at Heather. *I'll bet she'll join whichever side Ken is on.*

"Ken's right," Heather said. "It's better to be a little less rich and alive, than richer but dead."

"And as they say, you can't take it with you!" Elizabeth glowed with triumph. She'd won! "It's four against two, you guys," she said, looking at Jessica and Bruce. "Looks like you've been shot down."

"I can't believe what wimps you all are," Jessica exclaimed, stomping off toward her pack.

"You really *are* a boring nerd, Elizabeth Wakefield," Bruce said, stalking off into the night.

Elizabeth was stung by his harshness, but she dismissed it quickly. She wasn't the least bit surprised

114

that Bruce would want to throw caution to the wind and search for the last treasure. But she was annoyed that Jessica was being so immature about the whole thing. Jessica did make foolish choices sometimes, but she usually wised up if her life was at stake. *Could it be possible that Jess loves money more than life itself?* She shook her head at the thought.

It was a good thing that Ken and Todd listened to reason. Right now she was even grateful that Heather was so googly-eyed over Ken that she insisted on agreeing with everything he said.

"Your turn to build the fire, Miss Perfect. Didn't you want to do it last night?" Jessica asked, sounding snippy.

Why did Jessica have to be such an insufferable brat? The notion of building a campfire filled Elizabeth's already exhausted brain with dread. But she knew she had dug this hole for herself the night before. She almost wished she hadn't yelled at Bruce for saying that building fires was a man's job. Still, there was no way she was going to give Bruce or Jessica the satisfaction of not rising to the challenge.

"No prob," she said lightly. As the others proceeded to lay out their sleeping bags, Elizabeth ran through the techniques she'd learned over the weekend. She gathered some sticks and larger pieces of dry wood, piling them carefully to leave enough air between the pieces so the fire could breathe. She found some dry leaves and stuffed them under the pile to help ignite the wood.

But the leaves didn't seem to hold the spark. "Drat!" she said out loud as a cold gust of wind extinguished another match. It didn't help that her fingertips felt as if they were made of ice. After several more futile attempts, she'd gone through an entire book of matches. Elizabeth stood up, feeling her knees crack.

"Does anyone have a matchbook handy?" she asked casually.

"Having a little trouble, are you?" Bruce laughed and threw her a matchbook.

"Liz, do you need some help?" Todd asked.

"Elizabeth isn't your buddy, Todd," Jessica said quickly. "Your first responsibility is to see if your buddy needs help. And I do." Jessica was unfolding her air mattress.

"You're not going to get my help blowing up your air mattress, Jess. If the ground's not good enough for you, that's your problem," Todd said wearily. "Besides, I don't think Bruce would mind if I handled some of his buddy duties."

"Go right ahead, Wilkins. I'm not about to help Miss I-Am-Woman-Hear-Me-Roar Wakefield."

"I wasn't asking for your help, Bruce," Elizabeth said brusquely.

"Lighten up, Liz," said Todd, putting his arm around her shoulders. "Building a fire can be tricky. Don't think you have to prove anything to us."

"I'm not trying to *prove* anything, Todd. I can do this perfectly well by myself," she said, pulling out from under his arm.

Todd took a step back and looked at her.

"Are you OK?" he asked.

116

"Of course I'm OK. What, just because I want to build a fire you think there's something wrong with me?"

"It's not just the fire," he said, lowering his voice. "You just seem to be pulling away from me, or something."

"I don't need your help, Todd. Do you have a problem with that?" Elizabeth snapped. She was so tired and emotionally drained, she felt like bursting into tears.

"Fine, build the fire all by yourself. But hurry it up; we're hungry and cold," Todd said, a bit rudely.

She ignored him and went back to her task. *I'm not your damsel in distress, Todd Wilkins*, she silently fumed. *If it takes all night, I'm going to get this fire burning.*

"Well, I'm hungry now," Jessica complained.

"Maybe we should just eat tomorrow's ready-to-eat lunches instead of waiting for dinner to cook," suggested Ken. "I'm beat, and if I don't eat soon, I'm going to fall asleep with an empty stomach."

"Go ahead and eat. It's too late to roast hot dogs anyway," Elizabeth said.

Everyone pulled out their freeze-dried lunches and munched silently. The wind was really whipping now, blowing dirt and sand into Elizabeth's eyes. Her stomach growled loudly. She ignored her hunger and cold and scoured the area for more dried leaves. *I'm going to make this fire work.*

Many matches later Elizabeth finally got the wood to catch. She sat back on her heels, satisfied with the healthy flames. Elizabeth looked

117

up, expecting the others to comment on her fire. But no one congratulated her. They were all tucked into their sleeping bags, fast asleep. They hadn't bothered to write in their journals, Elizabeth realized, but she wasn't about to wake them.

She sighed and rummaged through her backpack for her journal and something to eat. Chewing on some dried apricots, she sat on a rock and balanced the pad on her knees. But when she reflected on the day, she felt overwhelmed by the idea of putting it all down on paper. Visions of almost suffocating in the mine shaft, finding gold, dreaming about fame, sweating under the hot sun, and her feelings about Bruce, all jumbled together in her mind. *I'm too tired to write, especially about all this. I'll catch up at some point tomorrow, after a good night's sleep,* she told herself.

Elizabeth crawled quietly into her sleeping bag, still wearing her T-shirt and shorts. She reached to zip up her bag, but the zipper was caught and wouldn't budge. After struggling for a while, she gave up and folded the top flap around her body, falling quickly asleep.

Chapter 7

Somebody, anybody, please let me out! Elizabeth thrashed and turned. Even in her sleep she realized she was just dreaming about being trapped in a meat locker, but she couldn't seem to wake herself up.

When she finally opened her eyes, she realized why the dream had felt so real. She was freezing. The fire had died out in the night, and somehow her sleeping bag had become further unzipped. Her T-shirt and shorts hadn't provided much warmth inside her drafty bed.

"What happened to the fire?" Heather asked groggily.

"I guess it wasn't strong enough to last the night," Elizabeth admitted.

"No wonder it's colder than Antarctica! Brrrrr!" Jessica burrowed down into her bag.

"It's not that easy building a fire, is it,

Wakefield?" Bruce said with obvious enjoyment.

"There wasn't enough dry wood around here," Elizabeth responded. She knew it was a lame excuse, but she couldn't resist defending herself against Bruce's provocation. She looked to the others for support.

"I see wood all over the place," Bruce said, rising up on his elbows. "In fact, I predict it'll take me no more than five minutes to build a fire so that we can at least have some hot oatmeal for breakfast." Bruce glanced at his high-tech digital watch and climbed out of his sleeping bag.

"Thanks, Bruce. We owe you one," said Todd.

Elizabeth caught Todd looking at her and shaking his head. She thought of how she had refused his help with the fire the night before, and she wondered whether he was still brooding over that. *That shouldn't have made him so mad—he's probably just grouchy because of the cold,* she decided.

Within minutes Bruce had started a roaring fire. They all ventured out of their bags to dress and get breakfast. Elizabeth gobbled some oatmeal while she planned the day's journey. With their dwindling water supply, finding a water source was the first priority. The map indicated a stream in the general direction they were going, although it looked pretty far away. She managed to calculate a route that would bring them there by nightfall. *At least I know I'm good at one thing,* she thought grimly.

After they'd eaten, they broke camp and divided the gold into six parts. *Nobody even mentioned leaving half the gold behind,* Elizabeth realized with a stab of guilt. But after the struggles of the day before and this morning's fire fiasco, she wasn't in the mood to have everyone yell at her again. So she said nothing and packed her stash.

Elizabeth was the first one to finish packing. She snapped the last buckle and heaved the pack onto her back.

"Yowww," she said out loud, reeling under the weight. Todd was just lifting his pack, and she noticed his knees were buckling underneath him, too.

"This extra gold sure adds weight, doesn't it?" she said.

"You got that right," Todd answered, adjusting his shoulder straps.

Bruce lifted his pack a few inches off the ground and dropped it. "Jeez. I'm not carrying that on my back," he said.

"What are you planning to do?" asked Jessica as she folded her pajamas into a pocket.

"I'm getting rid of some of these cans. Something's got to go, and it sure ain't the gold." With that Bruce started pulling out cans of beans and vegetables.

"Good idea," Todd said, shaking his pack off his back. "I never liked Spam, anyway."

Elizabeth watched with disbelief as everyone else started pulling cans from their packs.

"What are you doing? You're crazy!" she gasped.

"It's not a big deal," Ken said, sounding calm and relaxed. "We'll be at Desert Oasis tomorrow, and we have enough freeze-dried food to last us."

"But we were given strict rations. They figured out exactly how much food we would need," argued Elizabeth.

"Liz, I wish you would stop telling everyone what to do. If you don't want to take food out of your pack, don't," said Jessica.

"Yeah, if you're so hungry, feel free to take the leftovers." Bruce laughed and rolled a can over to Elizabeth.

"That's exactly what I'll do. You'll thank me for it when you're hungry for something hot tonight," Elizabeth retorted. She stuffed as many cans as she could fit into her pack.

The trail that morning led them through sand dunes. With her pack weighing her down, Elizabeth felt as if she were walking through quicksand. Her shoulders ached and her calves were killing her. Even worse, the wind kept blowing sand particles into her eyes.

Seeing Todd's brown head bobbing up and down a few yards in front of her, Elizabeth considered asking him to take some of the cans. Then she remembered how she had spurned his help the night before, and how he'd sat back and let her be flayed by Bruce this morning. *I can't possibly ask Todd for help,* she concluded. *Not now.*

Looking over her shoulder to see how Ken and Heather were doing, she saw a red stain on her shirt. Her shoulder straps had rubbed her skin raw! There was no doubt in her mind that she absolutely had to lighten her load.

Elizabeth considered her options. The most

sensible thing to do was to take out some of the gold. But if she took just a few of the cans out and kept some, she could probably carry the weight. *So I'll be a little hungry. It's not going to kill me,* she thought.

"I have to stop for a minute," she said, hoping Bruce would keep walking. To her dismay he stopped to watch her. She tried to ignore his snickers as she pulled items from her pack and placed them on the sand. Hating the thought of littering the desert, she turned away from the mess she'd made and lifted the pack on her back. *Much better.*

"When I've got my new school wardrobe picked out, I'll have to start shopping for my resort wear. You can't vacation in the Carribean without the proper attire," Jessica explained merrily to Todd.

Todd laughed. "No, that would be just wretched!"

Jessica knew Todd was teasing her, but she didn't care. Although she was still a little grumpy about not going after the final treasure, she'd decided to distract herself by focusing on her favorite topic—clothes.

"And I couldn't possibly drive a car without leather upholstery. I get a rash from vinyl," Todd joked.

Jessica noticed with surprise that she was actually having fun bantering with Todd. *Sometimes boring old Todd can actually be amusing,* she thought. *And he's got a cute smile.*

With her mind running down the list of bikinis, sarongs, and sundresses she'd need, Jessica didn't see Elizabeth in her path until she almost stepped on her.

"Liz! I'm sorry, I didn't see you." Elizabeth was crouched over the map.

"I'm just trying to figure out whether we're moving fast enough to get to tonight's camp," she explained.

"Well, you look exhausted. Has all that extra food weight tired you out?" Jessica asked, letting her satisfaction drip through her voice.

Elizabeth rubbed her shoulders tenderly. "My pack was so heavy, my shoulders started to bleed."

"Ouch," Jessica said in sympathy. She noticed the worried look on Todd's face, but he didn't say anything. *I guess he's not feeling too compassionate after Liz practically bit his head off about the fire last night. Serves her right.*

Elizabeth looked at the map and bit her lip. "I don't know whether it's best to head straight up this hill or walk around it. I'm so tired I can't even think. And Bruce isn't being the least bit helpful." Elizabeth shut her eyes and rubbed her temples. Jessica had never seen her sister look so defeated. She almost felt sorry for her. Almost.

"Do you want me to take over the navigation?" Todd offered. His empathy had obviously outweighed his annoyance.

"Oh, would you, Todd? I'd be so grateful," gushed Elizabeth. "I'll show you where we are, and where we need to go."

After Elizabeth had oriented Todd, they set off—Jessica and Todd were in front, and Bruce and Elizabeth pulled up the rear.

Jessica let her mind wander back to visions of designer swimwear until she noticed Todd fumbling with the map and compass. She flashed back to the precourse training and remembered that while Elizabeth had been hanging on every word of Kay's lessons about navigation, Todd had been busy designing new basketball plays. Jessica felt a flashbulb go off in her head. *This is my chance!*

"This navigation stuff is really tricky, isn't it?" Jessica said in her kindest voice. "Why don't you let me help you? After all, two heads are better than one."

"Umm, sure," Todd agreed, just as Jessica suspected he would. She took the map, at first pretending to be puzzled.

"I'm pretty sure we need to start veering left here," she said.

"Right." Todd nodded.

Jessica stifled a giggle. *Lucky for me, Todd can be the most gullible guy on earth.* She knew where she was leading them, and it wasn't to Desert Oasis. She was leading the group straight toward the final treasure.

Chapter 8

The hot sun beat down on top of Elizabeth's head. They'd left the sand dunes, but the ground was still dry and sparse. *I wish we could find some shade,* she thought desperately. She'd put on a fresh T-shirt, but it was already drenched with sweat.

From the ache in her stomach Elizabeth knew it was probably lunchtime. But she wasn't hungry; the heat had zapped her appetite. She'd missed dinner the night before and was so upset about her fire failure this morning that she'd just nibbled on her oatmeal. *If I don't eat soon, my stomach is going to start digesting its lining,* she thought ruefully.

"Is it time to stop for lunch yet, Todd?" Elizabeth called out.

"Why stop? Let's keep moving," Jessica responded. "I thought we were going to cut down on breaks, anyway."

"We have to take *some* breaks, Jess," Todd said.

"I could use some food," Ken added.

"Well, I guess we can afford a short break," Jessica acquiesced.

"I'm ready," Heather said, surreptitiously eyeing her wristwatch.

"If I see you turn on that stupid program, I swear I'll hurl that piece of junk TV over that ridge," warned Bruce.

"What's it to you, Patman? You don't have to watch," Heather shouted.

"Actually, Heather, maybe you shouldn't watch the show. You'll just get wrapped up, and we don't want to stop for too long," Ken said.

Heather fluttered her eyelashes. "You're right, Ken. When you put it like that, of course I understand," she said flirtatiously.

Elizabeth was losing more and more respect for Heather. But when she tried to catch Jessica's eye to show her compassion, Jessica looked quickly away. *I guess she's doing her best to ignore Heather,* Elizabeth thought. *Good for Jess.*

They settled down on a group of low rocks to eat. Elizabeth pulled out her lunch for the day—freeze-dried turkey and potato nuggets.

"Uhhh, Liz?" Todd asked tentatively. Elizabeth looked up, chewing on her food. "We all ate our lunches for dinner last night, while you were trying to light the fire. So maybe we could eat some of that canned food you've been carrying all morning?"

Elizabeth was torn. On the one hand, they'd

been the ones who were so quick to dump their food. She'd literally shed blood carrying those cans on her back—why should they benefit from her blood and sweat? But on the other hand, it *was* her fault that they hadn't had a hot dinner the night before.

Biting back the urge to say "I told you so," she nodded. "Sure, who'd like some semiwarm three-bean salad and corned-beef hash?" At least her pack would be that much lighter that afternoon.

They ate quickly and silently. Elizabeth had barely finished swallowing her last potato nugget when Jessica hustled them into action "Everybody ready? Let's move!"

Jess sure is impatient. Where is she getting her energy? Elizabeth wondered.

The trail continued to be completely absent of shade, but at least it was relatively flat and smooth as they followed the line of a canyon wall. As midday turned into afternoon, Elizabeth pulled out her sunglasses to keep out the glare. But as she settled them on her nose, she was puzzled. She could have sworn they were supposed to be heading northeast. The sun shouldn't have been in her eyes.

She asked Bruce what he thought.

"How should I know? Todd's the one who's supposed to be figuring that out."

Bruce was right. It was Todd's responsibility, and the last thing Elizabeth wanted to do was second-guess him after he'd been so nice about giving her a break. Besides, she was so hot and exhausted, she wouldn't have trusted herself to know right from left.

Elizabeth's confusion only intensified when Todd and Jessica veered up the side of the canyon. She was almost positive that the day's hike would remain flat; they weren't supposed to head over the hills until tomorrow. As the sun continued to drop in the sky, Elizabeth racked her brain to recall the course she'd plotted. Finally, she couldn't deny it any longer. They were supposed to be heading northeast through the flatlands, not northwest, right toward the mountains.

"Hold up!" she yelled. "Todd, where are you leading us?"

Todd stammered and mumbled. Finally he admitted that he'd been having trouble, so Jessica had offered to help him out.

"Why, is something wrong?" he asked innocently.

Elizabeth looked at Jessica, who bit her lip and looked away. Something was wrong. Very wrong.

"You're leading us to the next treasure, aren't you?" Elizabeth fumed.

"Was I?" Jessica asked sweetly. She twirled a strand of blond hair around her finger and smiled blandly.

"Don't play innocent with me, twin sister. You know exactly what you were doing."

"Awesome! Way to go!" Bruce cried, holding his right hand up for a high five.

Jessica slapped his hand with a mischievous

smile, infuriating Elizabeth all the more. *The nerve of those two!*

"Let me see if we can still get back on track," Elizabeth said. She grabbed the map and compass from Todd, who looked sheepishly at the ground. Doing some quick calculations, she surmised that if they were to backtrack, they'd never make it to the water supply. She spotted what looked like a stream of some sort winding through the foothills in the direction they were already headed. They needed water—tonight—so they had no choice but to continue.

"Even I'm surprised at your underhanded manipulation, Jessica Wakefield," Elizabeth scolded after she explained that they were now forced to follow Jessica's new plan. She felt her eyes burn with rage at the sight of her sister looking so smug and self-satisfied. She turned her attention to Todd.

"And you! I can't believe what an idiot you are for not being able to read a map—what were you doing during the lessons? Twiddling your thumbs? And how could you be stupid enough to turn over the responsibility to Jessica, of all people? You know how scheming she is!" Elizabeth's whole body shook with anger, and tears of frustration threatened to slide down her cheeks.

"I'm not going to stand here and let you call me an idiot, Elizabeth Wakefield," Todd said, his voice hard and strained. "I was doing you a favor, remember?"

"It's obvious now that your offer to help was

inspired by you wanting to pull some knight-in-shining-armor routine and come to my rescue. Unfortunately for the rest of us, you had no idea what you were doing!"

"I'm sick of your thinking you know what's best for everyone, and I know I'm not the only one here who feels that way," Todd yelled, looking around at the others.

"Yeah, Liz. Todd was just trying to help. You were the one who shirked your responsibility," Heather said in Todd's defense.

"Shirked my responsibility? I'm the only responsible person in this group of overgrown children." Elizabeth was so angry and disheartened at this point that she didn't know who deserved the most blame. She stared at each of them.

"Jessica, you're the most deceitful, untrustworthy person ever to walk on this planet. Todd, I can't believe how easily you were manipulated—you're weak and spineless." Elizabeth stopped and took a deep breath. She knew she should end her tirade, but the words seemed to force themselves out of her.

"Bruce, you think you're awesome, but you're just a no-good, egomaniacal buffoon," she continued. "Heather, you're nothing but a spoiled brat who can only be counted on to flirt with any guy in sight. And, Ken, I thought you were the one person here I could count on, but you're turning out to be absolutely worthless!"

Elizabeth felt her face flush with blood. Mindful of everyone's shocked expressions, she couldn't remember ever having felt so much hostility toward so many people at the same time.

"Deceitful," "spineless," "spoiled," "buffoon," "worthless." As the words she'd just hurled at her friends reverberated in her head, Elizabeth was surprised at their viciousness. She'd been angry before, but it wasn't like her to be so nasty. *Where did that come from?* she wondered.

With a sick feeling in the pit of her stomach, Elizabeth realized the source of her outburst. Deep down, she knew there was some truth to what Heather had said. She'd accepted the trust of the group to navigate that day, and she'd failed to live up to that trust. She could accuse and blame everyone else until she was blue in the face. It didn't change the fact that their current predicament was really her fault. After days of worrying about the rest of the group, she finally had to admit to herself that she was no more dependable than the rest of them.

Feeling the weight of the gold in her pack, Elizabeth wished she hadn't let greed overwhelm common sense that morning—she shouldn't have made her pack so heavy with gold. That's what had made her too tired to navigate. And with a stab of shame she thought of the cans of green beans and corned-beef hash that were now roasting in the hot sun, where she'd left them on the trail earlier in the day.

The gold. It's making us crazy. It was poisoning her mind, making her act totally out of character. Maybe she should take the treasure out of her pack right now. She could leave it there, so that she could focus on what was really important about the trip. Skills, teamwork, cooperation.

Then Elizabeth envisioned giving up the gold. At this point, would it really do any good? Besides, the rest of the group would just fight about how to split up her share. *No, I've carried it this far—it would be silly to throw it away now,* she rationalized.

Everyone stood around for a minute without saying anything.

Finally, Ken broke the ice. "Well, we're not going to solve anything if we just stand here throwing insults at each other. Let's keep hiking. Why don't you lead, Liz?"

They all looked at their feet as Elizabeth stomped to the front of the group and charged up the path. Jessica could tell that everyone else was just as taken aback by Elizabeth's behavior as she was. That ranting and raving version of Elizabeth Wakefield was a totally different person from her loving, eternally kind sister. *Was what I did so wrong?* Jessica asked herself.

It was true that she'd been deceitful. But only because Elizabeth had been so unreasonable about sticking to their route. Sometimes you just had to take life by the reins and go for it. That was the code Jessica lived by, and her life was a whole lot more fun than her boring sister's. Elizabeth's idea of adding excitement to her life was ordering her burger rare instead of well-done.

If her twin would just lighten up, she'd realize that they would make it back to Desert Oasis, no problem. And would it really be such a disaster if they didn't arrive at seven on the button? So they might get caught in a little rain. How serious was the storm forecast? Weather people were almost never right.

"Not a cloud in sight," Jessica said out loud. "No wind, either. I bet the storm is just a false alarm. This is the desert, after all. It hardly ever rains."

Todd, looking sullen, didn't respond. Glancing up the trail at the others, Jessica saw that no one was talking. Bruce hadn't said a thing when Elizabeth had insulted him, and now it seemed that he was imposing the silent treatment. Even Heather had lost her pep—she'd stopped batting her eyelashes at Ken. *What's going on with us?* Jessica wondered.

Before she had time to answer her own question, her thoughts were interrupted by a strange noise. It sounded as if a huge freeway were right over the next ridge. Jessica imagined herself sitting behind the wheel of a roomy, air-conditioned sedan with plush, velveteen seats. She'd turn up the stereo, lean back her seat, and head straight toward the ocean.

She stopped her daydream before she got too carried away. *It couldn't possibly be a freeway— we're out in the middle of nowhere,* she reminded herself. So what was it?

Up ahead Bruce and Elizabeth had stopped in their tracks. They seemed mesmerized by whatever was below them.

Jessica caught up with them and looked down. Cutting a sixty-foot ravine was a furious, rushing river—the water source that Elizabeth had recognized on the map.

"Gee, Liz, is that the 'stream' you saw on the map?" asked Jessica, happy to point out Elizabeth's error.

Todd shook his head. "I guess you're not the expert map reader you thought you were, Liz," Todd said nastily.

"At least I'm not totally incompetent," Elizabeth snapped, glaring at him.

Ken stepped between them. "Hold it, you guys. No matter who was wrong and who was right, we have no choice but to get across this river." Without another word Ken started down the slope. Along the way he grabbed hold of small shrubs to keep him from sliding all the way to the bottom. A few moments later everyone else followed.

When they reached water level, the fury of the river took Jessica's breath away. The roar of the rapids bounced off the canyon walls with a deafening impact. The huge angular boulders that disrupted the river's path spun water into whirlpools, sending chutes of foam, twigs, and small pebbles into the air. "How are we going to get across?" she cried.

"What about using that special arm-linking technique we learned in training? Seems like an emergency river crossing is just what they had in mind when they taught it to us," Todd suggested.

"Good idea," Ken said. Assuming his natural

role as quarterback, Ken developed the strategy and laid it out for the rest.

"Since I'm the strongest guy here, I'll lead. Now, we should go guy-girl-guy-girl, so one girl needs to go on the end." He paused, and his eyes met Jessica's. "Jess, you're the strongest girl here, so you can handle the end."

Jessica nodded mutely.

"Todd's stronger than Bruce, so he should go next to you. Elizabeth, you go on the other side of Todd, then Bruce, then Heather will be between me and Bruce."

As the water raged beside them, Ken, Heather, Bruce, Elizabeth, Todd, and Jessica lined up one by one and locked arms. But as they headed for the river, seeing Heather cower next to Ken was more than Jessica could tolerate. *I should be next to my boyfriend during this life-threatening ordeal, not Heather,* she thought.

Up to her knees now in water, Jessica broke out of her lock with Todd and rushed to the front of the line, forcing herself between Ken and Heather.

"Jessica, you're messing up the balance!" Ken yelled as Heather screamed.

"We may not survive this, and I want to spend my last moments at your side," Jessica said, gripping him tighter.

"Bruce, Heather, try to switch places," Ken shouted, his voice barely audible over the noise of the rapids and Heather's cries.

"I can't let go!" Heather yelled. She seemed

paralyzed with fear and wouldn't let go of either Bruce or Jessica.

"OK, Jessica. You just better hang on to Heather with all your strength," commanded Ken. They'd gotten up to their waists, but the riverbed seemed to have leveled off. They started moving again toward the opposite shore. Jessica gripped Heather tightly as the water pushed against her body.

After a minute Jessica noticed that Heather was not returning her grip.

"Heather, hold on to me!" she yelled out.

"I'm scared!" came Heather's weak reply.

The water tugged and pulled. Then Jessica felt Heather tremble violently and realized she'd started to panic. Just as she was about to alert Bruce, Jessica felt Heather's arms go limp and start to slip from her grasp. She tried to hold her tighter, but Heather's arm was wet and slippery. Before she could do anything to stop her, Heather slipped through her fingers.

"Help me!" Heather screamed, her voice hysterical.

Jessica instinctively grabbed for Bruce as the rapids whisked Heather away.

Chapter 9

"Ken, stop! Heather's gone down the river!" Jessica
shouted at the top of her lungs. "What do we do?"

Ken turned to see Heather's blond head bobbing and bouncing in the white foam.

"We can't do anything for her until we get to
land!" Ken hollered, tugging harder to speed their
crossing. He tried not to think about Heather floating
downstream. Considering the strength of the current
swirling around his legs, her chances didn't look good.

The shore was only about ten yards away now,
but it took all of Ken's strength to keep the group
moving through the rapids. The slick rocks in the
riverbed were treacherous—he kept slipping, getting more and more of his backpack wet.

All of a sudden Ken heard Elizabeth scream.

"It's OK, I just tripped. I'm OK," Elizabeth
called out when the others stopped to see what had
happened.

"Could you try not to scream like that?" Todd yelled. "We're tense enough!"

"I'm sorry. I couldn't help it."

"Be careful, everyone. Move quickly, but be careful," urged Ken. "We're almost there."

Finally, Ken passed the worst of the rapids. With his footing more sure, he used his upper-body strength to pull Jessica, Bruce, Elizabeth, and Todd to dry land. "Now we've got to rescue Heather!"

"Let's go," Elizabeth agreed.

Without stopping to catch their breath, they dropped their packs and raced down the riverbank. Grabbing branches and loose sticks along the way, they scrambled through the brush, jumping over mud and rocks. Suddenly Ken spotted Heather's blond head in the water.

"Heather!" Elizabeth screamed, waving her arms.

"Help me!" Heather wailed. She was holding on to a large log near the shore.

"Hold on, we'll get you out!" Ken yelled.

Jessica offered the few sticks she'd managed to scrounge.

"We can't pull her out with these," he spit out as he tossed them aside. "You've helped enough," he said sarcastically.

Jessica stepped back, silenced.

"Hold on to me—let's form a chain," Ken ordered, climbing out toward the log. Bruce wrapped his arms around Ken's waist, and Todd anchored them.

"Grab hold of my hand!" Ken screamed, reaching his arm out.

Heather clutched the log. "I can't let go," she screamed. "The river is pulling me away!"

Looking down, Ken saw Heather's legs whipping out under the log.

"Guys, give me some more slack—I have to grab Heather's arm!" he told them. Elizabeth grabbed Todd around the waist to steady him in the mud, and Todd and Bruce inched forward. Ken reached down and locked his fingers onto Heather's biceps. "Gotcha!" he cried. "Now, on my count, we'll pull you out of there. Ready?"

Heather nodded weakly.

"OK. One, two, three!" Feeling Bruce's arms wrapped tightly around his waist, Ken pulled with all his might. He heaved Heather upward, falling back against Bruce and Todd onto the shore. Heather collapsed onto the mud and gravel riverbank. Between sobs of gratitude and exhaustion, she asked if they'd rescued her pack and gear.

"We were too busy making sure you were still alive to worry about your stuff, Heather," Ken said.

"But it had everything—my clothes, my TV . . . my *gold*! All my gold is gone!" she said, weeping into her hands. Then she looked up. "Jessica Wakefield, you owe me. This is all your fault. I bet you planned it all along."

Jessica gasped. "How dare you accuse me—you sniveling crybaby."

"Maybe you didn't plan it, Jess, but you sure

can take the credit for putting Heather's life in danger," Ken said, his tone harsh.

"What are you talking about? Heather was the one who didn't hold on. Her wrists turned to noodles and she slithered out of our grasp, right, Bruce?"

"Nice try, Wakefield. The least you can do is stand up and accept the blame," Heather said.

"Actually, Heather, Jessica's right," Bruce admitted. "I was holding on to you as hard as I could, but you let go."

"But . . . I—" she sputtered. "Well, I never," she said finally, crossing her arms in front of her.

"However it happened, if Jessica hadn't gone and broken up the chain right in the middle of the river, Heather wouldn't have panicked, and everything would be fine," Ken stated, giving Jessica a meaningful glare.

"I don't think it should be a criminal offense to want to be next to my boyfriend in times of danger," Jessica said hotly.

"That is so childish, Jessica," Heather sneered. Ken looked at his girlfriend, who was pouting and sulking. *Heather's right. You're being totally childish,* he wanted to say.

"If you really loved me, Ken, you wouldn't let her talk to me like this," Jessica said plaintively.

"Maybe I agree with her," Ken retorted.

Jessica stared at Ken, her mouth gaping open. "I will never forgive you for this, Ken Matthews!" Jessica raged, and she stormed off downstream. After a moment Elizabeth followed her.

142

"Sure, go after your stupid sister," Todd said, shaking his head.

"What is with those Wakefield women that makes them think they're better than everybody?" Ken asked as he watched the two blond heads disappear down the riverbank. *I really thought Jessica and I had something special,* he thought. *But she's turning out to be more trouble than she's worth.*

"Let's head back up to where we left our packs. Heather, you need some help walking?" Ken offered.

"Oh, yes," Heather said gratefully, throwing her arms around his shoulders.

As they turned away from the rushing river, something blue caught Todd's eye. "Hold up!" he said, jogging toward the water's edge. "Hey, Heather! Here's your sleeping bag." The sleeping bag had come loose from Heather's backpack and gotten tangled in a pile of twigs next to the shore. It was sopping wet, but it seemed to be intact. Todd leaned out over the water and grabbed it. "I've got it!" he shouted to the others.

"Oh, terrific," Heather said flatly. "Now I can sleep in a wet bag that'll probably freeze into a giant ice cube in the middle of the night." She took what was left of her gear from Todd with barely disguised disdain.

"It'll dry," Todd answered. "We'll keep it by the fire tonight. In the meantime we'll figure out a way to keep you warm tonight."

Heather raised her eyebrows and smiled. "Promises, promises," she said.

Todd blushed as the four headed upstream. He walked behind Heather and Ken as they struggled their way up the jagged riverbank. Waist-high shrubs grabbed at Todd's shirt and poked his shins.

"I guess this is as good a place as any to set up camp," Todd said when they finally got back to their packs. "What do you say we get a fire going, Bruce?"

"Sure, Wilkins. You've come to the expert," Bruce joked. While Ken helped Heather dry off and find some fresh clothes, Bruce and Todd started on the fire.

The only wood they found was small chips and sticks that had been thrown from the river and dried in the sun. They gathered a large pile, but there weren't enough dried leaves to get any piece of wood to spark.

"How about all that paper in those dumb journals? I know I'm not going to fill mine from cover to cover," Bruce suggested.

"Why not?" said Todd. He wasn't going to fill the whole thing, either. Getting a good fire going was a lot more important to survival than scribbling about his innermost thoughts. *Liz wouldn't approve, but I don't care,* Todd thought, smiling to himself.

"I wonder where your girlfriend and the other brat ran off to," Bruce mused, stuffing wads of paper underneath the wood.

"Can it, Patman," Todd said, ducking out of Bruce's reach. But he laughed despite himself. *Whatever happened between Liz and Bruce in that cave is over now,* Todd realized.

Bruce held a match under the paper, and the spark caught quickly. In minutes they had a robust fire.

"Great going, you guys. C'mon, Heather, let's heat up by the fire," Ken said.

"How'd you get it to be that gorgeous orangey color?" Heather asked.

"Vell, you zee, vee added zome mageek fire dust, giving zee lovely glow you zee here," Todd faked a pathetic French accent.

"Give me a break." Elizabeth laughed. She'd just appeared at the camp, dragging a sullen Jessica behind her. Immediately the relaxed mood shifted.

"So the Wakefield royals have deigned to share their aura with us," said Bruce, looking straight at Elizabeth. "We're so very honored, aren't we?"

Ken ignored Bruce and asked if they were OK.

"We're fine, just a little damp, right, Jess?"

Jessica just grunted. Elizabeth looked around at the group.

"This fire is absolutely gorgeous—I guess the wood around here burns differently. And it's so nice and warm," Elizabeth prattled on. "Why don't we all change out of our wet clothes? I think I still have one more clean set of sweats that would feel scrumptious right about now." Elizabeth bounced over to her backpack.

Todd knew that Elizabeth was trying to bring a sense of camaraderie back to the splintered group, but it was too late—for him, anyway. The words "weak" and "spineless" echoed in his head.

"Elizabeth's right about changing out of these disgusting clothes. Ken's being so nice to lend me a dry outfit," Heather gushed, taunting Jessica by holding up Ken's polo shirt and sweatpants.

Her mouth set in a grimace, Jessica yanked a brush through her damp hair.

"Now I could use some help getting out of my sh— Ohmigosh! My shoes are ruined! These are custom-made, and now they're ruined," Heather wailed.

Jessica laughed loudly. "I hear the lost colony of Atlantis needs a new cheerleading squad for its water-polo team," she said, putting her brush down. When Bruce laughed, Heather nearly burst into tears.

"Jessica, don't you know when it's time to stop? Heather almost lost her life. Stop being such a total jerk, especially since you're the one who put us all in danger." Ken stroked Heather's shoulders protectively.

Todd looked from Ken to Jessica and saw her surreptitiously wipe at her eyes with a clenched fist. "We're all obviously a little wound up. Let's just get dried off and calm down," Todd said.

"Todd's right. We're all safe now, so let's just get warm," Elizabeth agreed.

Ken looked from Elizabeth to Todd with an expression of shock on his face. "I can't believe you guys are just dismissing this as if it was nothing. I'll be the first to admit that crossing the river shook me up a lot. Heather almost drowned. We almost *lost* a member of the group," he yelled.

"And I think it's best that we not dwell on it, Ken," said Elizabeth, nodding her head in Heather's direction.

Ken shook his head vigorously. "Don't you guys realize what's happening to us? We're acting like nothing we do is real, as if there's someone who will always pull us out of danger. We rescued Heather, but she could just as easily have been pulverized in the rapids. It was pure luck that she got caught on that fallen log."

Todd looked over at Heather. She sat on a rock, her knees hugged close to her chest, rocking slowly back and forth. She was obviously unnerved. The last thing she needed right now was the reminder that she'd almost died.

"Maybe we should just drop this, Ken," he said out loud.

"Drop this? Pretend it didn't happen?" Ken asked. "This isn't an amusement park—the ride doesn't end when the operator pulls the switch. This is real." They all looked down at their feet.

"What's the use, Matthews? Let's get dinner going. I'm starving," Bruce said, shrugging.

"Really, Ken, Heather's fine, everybody's fine. This wasn't the first scare we've had, and we've managed to get through everything OK," said Elizabeth.

Todd looked at Elizabeth in surprise. He'd expected her to join with Ken and launch into one of her sermons. But she was engrossed in untying her wet shoelaces. *Liz usually loves to discuss and dissect intense experiences*, Todd thought, *running them into the ground until they just about lose all their meaning.*

Ken threw up his hands. "Fine. I give up," he said, going to his pack to pull out his dinner.

"Oh, no!" said Elizabeth all of a sudden. She was digging around in her pack.

"What is it?" asked Ken.

"I can't find the water-purification kit. I think I left it on the trail."

"Good going, Wakefield," Bruce said. "Now we'll all catch bacteria, get sick, and die."

"I just can't believe I left it," said Elizabeth, still searching fruitlessly. "The heat must have melted my brain."

"Don't worry about it. Let's just fill our canteens and hope for the best," said Ken.

Liz is sure letting us down, thought Todd, watching Elizabeth and Ken make their way to the river. With a long stick he poked and prodded at the burning wood of the fire, watching the fierce, angry flames. *At least we avoided another argument,* he thought glumly.

Suddenly, with a loud crack, one log split, sending the flames jumping and flashing as the fire settled down again. When one log started to roll away, Todd reached to stop it with his bare hand. "Owww!" he gasped, shaking his wrist. *What was I thinking, using my bare hand to grasp a burning piece of wood?*

Ken's words came back to him. *This isn't an amusement park—this is real.* The heat of the fire was real, just as Heather's near-death experience

148

was real. Todd himself had almost lost his life just yesterday, and now that experience felt like a distant memory.

Reflecting on the past couple of days, Todd ran through visions of the collapsing mine shaft, finding the gold, the river crossing, and the stories Elizabeth had told him about people dying in Death Valley. At every turn somebody in their group seemed to be in grave danger, and they plodded along as if nothing had happened.

Were they ignoring the reality of their experience? Were they so jaded by television and movies that this whole trip seemed like a story happening to someone else? *I just hope this story doesn't end up a Movie of the Week called* The Tragedy of the Sweet Valley High Six, he thought darkly.

Everyone chewed quietly on their dinners of toasted tortillas and melted freeze-dried cheese as the fire crackled and crickets chirped. Jessica was still brooding, and Ken was sitting with Heather. Elizabeth noticed that Todd was sitting on a rock by himself, just outside the group. *Maybe now's the perfect time to make up with Todd,* she decided.

"Care for some company?" she asked brightly, walking over to him. He looked up and shrugged his shoulders. *OK, so I'll be the one to swallow my pride and apologize first.* She sat down and turned to Todd, ready to apologize for being so disagreeable—first about his offer of help with the fire, and then about his goof-up with the map reading.

149

But when she turned her head to face him, something strange caught her eye. Over Todd's shoulder, not twenty feet from where they'd set up camp, Elizabeth saw what looked like remnants of a fire.

"What's this?" she said out loud, getting up to investigate further. Todd followed her, and they bent to scope out the pile of ashes. They were fresh!

"Maybe it's the escaped convicts," Bruce said after Elizabeth alerted them. Everyone laughed nervously. Everyone except Heather.

"I told you! I told you they were near! Nobody believed me. Now what are we going to do?"

"We're not going to do anything, Heather. Lots of people camp in Death Valley. In fact, I'm surprised we haven't run across another group of hikers yet," reassured Ken.

"Don't be a doofus, Matthews. No one in his right mind actually chooses to camp in this odious place," Bruce observed. He paused for effect and said in a low voice, "I'll bet the convicts slept in this very spot just last night!" Heather gasped.

"Stop it, Bruce. Don't make this worse," Elizabeth cautioned. But she couldn't help wondering if he was right.

"Give me a break," said Jessica, going back to where she'd left her half-eaten dinner.

Todd sat down on his lonely perch and picked up his meal. Elizabeth watched him pointedly avoid her gaze and realized that the moment to mend their relationship had passed. *Be that way,* she told him in her mind. *I'm glad I get the chance to apologize—you're the one who's been acting so juvenile.* She decided to wait it out. Sooner or later he'd come crawling back for forgiveness.

After they'd eaten, Elizabeth realized she had let the whole day go by without writing her journal entry for the previous night. *I wish I'd known today was going to be this hectic—I'll never have enough energy to write all this down,* she thought. When she reminded the group it was time to write in their journals, Bruce and Todd looked at each other and chuckled mysteriously.

"What's that all about?" Elizabeth asked.

"Oh, nothing," said Bruce. "Todd and I were just discussing how we would have liked to catch the Lakers game tonight after dinner. Too bad Heather went and lost her TV."

"Bruce Patman, that's about the most insensitive thing I've ever heard you say!" Heather said, her eyes welling up with tears.

"Just yanking your chain, Mallone. You make it so easy," said Bruce, laughing.

"Lay off her, Bruce," Ken said, coming to Heather's defense.

Jessica pulled her journal out of her pack, zipping the pocket closed with a loud rip. "I've got lots to write about tonight," she said, eyeing Ken. "Consider yourself lucky that you'll never see it, Ken Matthews."

Elizabeth pulled out her own notebook. *There should be a lot of interesting journal entries tonight,* she thought with a sigh.

Chapter 10

Heather's Journal
Death Valley Adventure Trek
Day 3

Today was the most terrifying day of my life. I thought for sure I was going to die in that horrible river. And it's all Jessica's fault! I always knew she was an immature and stupid girl, but this latest move has surpassed even my own expectations. I don't care what she says, Jessica let go of me, not the other way around. I can't believe Bruce actually stuck up for her. I did not let go—what was I supposed to do when Jessica squirmed her way next to Ken and let me fend for myself against the raging river? I swear Jessica will pay for making me lose all my stuff. She shouldn't just give me half her gold, she should give me all of it.

At least my plot to make Ken fall in love with me seems to be coming along right on track. One more of Jessica's stupid stunts, and I won't even have to flirt. He'll just come begging to be my boyfriend. Maybe I'll string him along for a while, just to make him that much more grateful when I do allow him to go out with me. Actually, I think tonight's the night to make my move.

Ken's Journal
Death Valley Adventure Trek
Day 3

I'm sitting here trying to remember how I fell in love with Jessica, but it feels like I was a whole different Ken when it happened. That old Ken thought she was so cute and fun— now I only see how selfish and infantile she really is. What a disappointment that is—I really thought she was something special.

Speaking of special, I've always had so much respect for Elizabeth. I couldn't believe it when she just dismissed our terrifying experience at the river as no big deal. Was she just defending her sister? Or is she a lot more irresponsible than she lets on?

Jessica's Journal
Death Valley Adventure Trek
Day 3

I've never felt so betrayed in all my life. I can't believe that Ken didn't even care about being next to me when we crossed that river. Not only didn't he want to be next to me, he put me all the way on the other end, as far away from him as possible. I thought he really loved me, but I guess he just wanted me to be his girlfriend when it suited him.

And Heather! I thought I hated her before, but now I think she's so vile, she's sub-human. I bet she's an alien in disguise, from a planet where all the people are weak, scheming, low-down, and evil. I was using all my strength to hold on to her, and she blames it on me! And now she's using that to steal Ken.

Actually, now that I think about it, I don't want Ken to be my boyfriend, anyway. If he likes the weak, needy, helpless kind of woman that Heather Mallone is, then he sure doesn't deserve me. Good riddance is all I can say. But first, I'll rub it in his face. He needs a taste of his own medicine.

Elizabeth's Journal
Death Valley Adventure Trek
Day 3

Jessica looked so hurt and alone tonight, I almost feel sorry for her. But pulling that stunt in the river was incredibly stupid. I have to agree with Ken that if she hadn't done that, we would have gotten across the river with no problem. Come to think of it, the fact that we were even faced with the treacherous river is really all Jessica's fault. The group had made a democratic decision—the right one—and Jessica undermined it. But, actually, I have to give Bruce some blame for Jessica's foolishness. Jessica would never have gone to such deceitful extremes if greedy and pigheaded Bruce weren't there to back her up. Now that I'm on the topic of spreading blame, Todd sure deserves a lot of it. He should never have offered to take over the navigation when he didn't even know what he was doing. And he of all people should know how Jessica gets when she has an idea in her head. To trust her was pure lunacy.

I still haven't even written about yesterday's events. How am I ever going to get this story published if I don't keep track of every detail? Actually, considering the turns this trip has taken, maybe I should fictionalize my account. I'd be embarrassed to publicize this disaster of an adventure trek. We're all behaving so horribly. I can't believe I took the food out of my pack to make room for the gold. What has come over me?

Todd's Journal
Death Valley Adventure Trek
Day 3

I just know Liz was coming over to apologize at dinner, but I'm glad she noticed the ashes before she had the chance. I had absolutely no intention of forgiving her, but sometimes I can't help it when she looks at me with those beautiful blue eyes. I'm still angry at her, and I'm not about to tell her I'm sorry. So I guess it's better to just avoid her for a while.

Maybe it would be a good thing if she and Bruce did get together. On second thought, scratch that idea. It would be awful!

Bruce's Journal
Death Valley Adventure Trek
Day 3

This journal thing is so stupid. I don't even know what to write about. I just read over what I wrote the other night, and I feel pretty much the same. Except that I'm psyched that we found gold. What's there to write about that? I'm psyched. It's way cool. If we hadn't found the gold, I'd still think this trip was just a huge waste of time. And now it's gotten even worse! I'm the only one here who hasn't gone completely wacko. They're all getting riled up about such stupid things, while I'm staying focused on something much more important—gold. Even Heather, who I used to think was hot, is really just as much of a weak loser as the rest. Once this trip is over, I'm never hanging out with these people again!

Chapter 11

"Don't tell me Bruce Patman is actually getting deep and reflective in his old age," Jessica teased as she lowered herself onto the ground next to Bruce, who was leaning against a tree. "Whatcha writing?" she asked, peering over his notebook.

"Do you mind?" Bruce shielded the pages from her view.

"OK, OK," she said, backing off. "What did you write, anyway? It must be really interesting. . . ." Jessica's eyes glittered with curiousity.

"None of your business," Bruce said dismissively.

"Did you write anything about me?" Jessica asked, turning up the corners of her mouth.

Bruce narrowed his eyes. He hated it when Jessica flashed her dimples at him, because he knew exactly what it meant: She wanted something from him. And he was a sucker for dimples.

"What do you want, Wakefield?"

"What do you mean, what do I want? Can't I just want to talk to you? I thought we were friends," Jessica pouted. Then her mouth drew into a tight line. "Can you believe how timid these people are? I'm glad I have one ally in the search for the gold," she said, patting his arm amiably.

"Yeah, they're pretty dopey," Bruce agreed, looking at the long fingers that were now resting on his hand. *What is going on here—first Elizabeth, now Jessica?* he wondered. For a long time he and Jessica had had a mutual understanding—they would tolerate each other, as long as they didn't talk any more than was absolutely necessary. Jessica stared at him squarely, a picture of innocence and sincerity.

Then he saw her eyes wander across the campsite and flash with fury. He followed her gaze and saw Heather and Ken resting against a couple of the backpacks. Heather whispered something to Ken, and a second later they both broke out into laughter. Bruce felt as if he'd been hit over the head with a hammer. *I get it. She wants to make her little boyfriend jealous.*

His first reaction was anger—he hated to be used. Then he thought again. *If it means I might get to have some fun out here, I'll play along.* But not without first letting Jessica know he knew what was going on.

"Looks like Ken is falling hard for our Miss Mallone," he said, smirking.

Without missing a beat Jessica hissed, "Don't

they just deserve each other?" Then she sighed. "I really thought Ken was special, but I guess I was wrong." She shook her head slowly, then closed her fingers around Bruce's hand. "That's what I like about you, Bruce."

"What are you talking about?" Bruce held his hand still, not sure whether or not to return Jessica's grip.

"You're consistent, you're true to yourself." Bruce let out a guffaw. "No, I'm serious," Jessica persisted. "OK, I admit it, sometimes you make me so mad I want to strangle you. But at least I always know what to expect from you. I hate guys who act so sweet one minute, then turn around and betray you behind your back," she said, looking straight at Ken.

Bruce studied Jessica's face. The light of the fire jumped and bounced, revealing gold and glittery strands in her blond hair and a well of tears in her eyes. Squeezing her hand, Bruce felt his heart skip a beat. There was a time long ago when he'd wanted Jessica—wanted her spark, her fire. That old attraction surged through him now.

She turned to face him. Bruce took a deep breath. He wanted to kiss her. Right there, right now. He didn't care who saw.

"Where am I going to sleep? My sleeping bag is still a soggy mess," Heather cried, looking forlorn.

Jessica blinked and pulled her hand away from Bruce's. Heather had broken the spell, but Jessica had come very close to kissing Bruce. And not just

161

out of spite against Ken. *I actually* wanted *to kiss Bruce Patman,* she pondered disbelievingly. *Have I gone nuts?*

Jessica stood up abruptly, noticing with satisfaction that Ken was watching her with a puzzled expression on his face. *Well, at least he noticed,* she thought. When she caught his eye, she smiled smugly.

"We all have extra blankets—we can put together a makeshift bed for Heather," Ken said, averting his eyes from Jessica.

"Sure, Heather, you can have my blanket," Elizabeth added, looking up from her journal.

"Mine, too," said Todd, tossing his gray army blanket over to Heather.

Jessica burned as she watched everyone rally around Heather. *If anyone so much as suggests I do anything for that shrew, I'll tell them where they can shove their blanket.* To avoid the possibility, Jessica took the opportunity to head down to the riverbank to wash up before bed.

But as soon as she splashed cold water onto her face, she was struck like a slap in the face by an even more chilling thought: *Heather's going to steal my gold while I sleep!* Heather *was* under the delusion that she was entitled to some of Jessica's gold, and robbing Jessica in the dead of night was just her style. So Jessica cut her routine short and raced back up to camp. On the way she passed everyone else going down to the river.

Jessica rubbed her eyes. "G'night, everyone—I'll probably be knocked out by the time you're back."

Jessica faked a yawn, complete with a stretch.

"Good night, Jess," said Elizabeth icily. The rest of the group just grunted. Their rudeness wasn't lost on Jessica, but she didn't care. *If I never speak to any of these traitors again, I'll be happy*, she told herself. Then she caught Bruce giving her a meaningful look as he dropped some more wood onto the fire as he made his way down to the river. He stopped and faced her, opening his mouth as if to say something. But no words came out. He drew his hand slowly through his dark hair, his cheeks glowing red in the fire. Was he blushing, or just hot?

"Good night," he said quickly. Then he turned and walked away.

Why do I think Bruce is looking so cute tonight? Jessica wondered as she watched him disappear into the darkness.

Pushing thoughts of Bruce aside, Jessica hurried over to her pack and dug out the plastic bag that held her gold. Stuffing it down into the foot of her sleeping bag, she crawled inside and felt her heartbeat slow down immediately as she nestled her prized package between her toes. She closed her eyes and pretended to be asleep when she heard the others come back to bed.

Through lidded eyes she noticed that Bruce had pulled his sleeping bag really close to hers—so close, she could smell his shampoo. She rolled herself closer still. In the dark night, it felt nice to have his strong body next to hers.

❖   ❖   ❖

Ken had just started to dream. He was in a huddle, calling plays to his running back. But his coach kept making fun of his calls. Then he realized the voice didn't belong to his coach. It was Jessica. Jessica was on the field, yelling through her megaphone.

"Ken Matthews! Are you a quarterback or a wimp?" Everyone in the bleachers laughed. Ken burned with embarrassment. Jessica raised the megaphone to her mouth again.

"Ken! Are you awake?" Ken felt something brush his cheek. *Wait. This isn't a dream.* He opened his eyes and saw Heather looking down at him.

"I'm sorry I woke you up, but you were really tossing and turning. It looked like you were having a bad dream," she said tenderly.

"Yeah, I guess I was," Ken mumbled.

"Do you want to talk about it?" With her thick hair all pulled back into a French braid, Heather's face looked fresh and sweet. She smiled warmly. Ken looked over to where Jessica had laid out her sleeping bag. She was cuddling up against Bruce! Ken rubbed his eyes with the back of his knuckles.

"Let's go talk," Heather said. "Come on. They're all asleep." She wriggled out of her sleeping bag and held her hand out for Ken to follow.

Hand in hand, Ken and Heather crept quietly away from the fire, trying not to crunch the leaves on the ground. A cool wind whipped around them, so they found a rock to use as shelter just outside the halo of light from the fire. They settled on the ground.

"What were you dreaming about?" Heather said in a whisper.

"Ummm. Well. It was kind of weird," Ken said, keeping his eyes on his hands.

"Was it about Jessica?" Heather asked innocently.

"Yeah, it was," Ken said, startled. "How'd you know?"

"Well, I couldn't help but notice that you two seem to be having some problems." When Ken didn't respond, Heather continued. "If you ask me, I think she's insanely jealous, and she's worried that you're going to fall in love with me. It's really sad that girls get so competitive with each other," she said, shaking her head.

"Totally—I know what you mean," Ken said. "She wouldn't get off my case. I mean, I kept telling her she had no reason to be jealous." Ken looked at Heather and sucked in his breath. He could smell the fresh scent of her face soap.

"Doesn't she?" she asked, taking one of his hands.

Don't do it! screamed a voice at the back of Ken's head. *Why not? I've lost Jessica anyway,* he responded to the voice. He gripped Heather's hand tightly, running his other hand around the back of her neck. He pulled her face to him and closed his eyes. Then he felt her warm, soft lips meet his.

In the middle of the night Jessica woke up.

There was one part of her nightly routine she shouldn't have skipped—she had to go to the bathroom. She rolled over onto her belly, bumping up against a body. "Oops!"

"Hrmphhd." Bruce's sleeping face was two inches away. He smacked his lips in his sleep. There was drool on his cheek. *Gross. Bruce is revolting,* Jessica told herself. *I was out of my mind for even thinking that I wanted to kiss him.*

Jessica sneaked out of her sleeping bag, grabbed her flashlight, and crept away by the light of the fire. Once out of sight range, she switched on her flashlight to light her path.

"Yikes!" she gasped. A lizard scurried across her feet; the beam of her flashlight had startled it. Once she caught her breath, Jessica shone her flashlight around the area. *This place sure looks different at night,* she thought. The land that had seemed so barren and uninhabited during the day was alive with movement and sound under the cloak of darkness. Jessica thought back to Kay's lecture on desert life and remembered learning that most animals in the desert are nocturnal.

Once she got over her initial skittishness, Jessica was fascinated with the movements of the night. She found herself wandering farther and farther downstream, listening to the ribbets of the frogs, the fish splash in the water, insects buzzing around her head. The moon hung heavy and full over the hills in the distance, glowing iridescent white. Moonlight bounced off the rushing river, and the wet rocks glistened. Entranced, Jessica lost track of time until the hoot of an owl startled the spell. *Whoops! I'd better get back to bed.*

She retraced her steps and got to the camp, where the fire still glowed with a warm orange light. Jessica shut off her flashlight and snuggled back into her sleeping bag. *That's funny,* she thought as she pulled the top flap back. *I thought I had zipped it closed when I left.*

Her eyes opened wide as she remembered her gold. Turning on her flashlight, she pulled the flap of her sleeping bag all the way back. It was empty. Her gold stash was gone!

Elizabeth woke up to the sound of Jessica's screams.

"My gold is gone!" she yelled. "Someone stole my gold!" Elizabeth rubbed her eyes and saw Jessica frantically shaking her sleeping bag inside out.

"What are you—" Elizabeth started to say. Just then Heather appeared from the darkness.

"Heather, you no-good thief, you took my gold," Jessica accused.

"Oh, Jessica, stop your insane ravings. I didn't take anything," said Heather, calmly returning to her bed. "Not that I don't deserve it."

"You're never going to get away with this, Heather—I'm onto you," Jessica continued.

"Jess, I'm sorry to say that it was impossible for me to have stolen your precious treasure. I was otherwise occupied," she said, smiling. Then Ken walked into the light.

"Heather's right," he said sheepishly. "She was with me."

Jessica looked from Ken to Heather and back to Ken. Then she flashed Heather a look of unadulterated hatred. Jessica's hands clenched into fists, and Elizabeth could see her chest swell with fury. *Now I understand what they mean by, "If looks could kill,"* thought Elizabeth. *This is going to get ugly.*

"Everybody calm down," Bruce said, breaking the tension of the moment. "It's obvious that one of us has Jessica's gold. So whoever took it, fess up now." No one spoke up.

"The only thing left to do is for everyone to empty their packs," said Todd. "That means you, too, Liz."

Elizabeth looked at him in shock; she couldn't believe the coldness in his voice. *Now I'm even more glad I didn't have the opportunity to apologize to Todd last night,* she thought. *He doesn't deserve my compassion!*

Bruce grumbled louder than the rest, but everyone finally cooperated. With all their belongings laid out around the fire, Todd counted only four sacks of gold nuggets. Jessica's was still missing.

"Whoever stole it just hid it somewhere else," cried Jessica.

"Or maybe the escaped convicts got it," Bruce said lightly. No one laughed.

"That's it! The convicts discovered your gold!" screeched Heather. "They're total sneaks—they knew we found treasure, so they've been following us!"

168

"Nice try, Heather. Go blame your crime on some made-up story about convicts," Jessica snapped.

"I'm not making it up. We all heard it on the news. Our lives are in danger!"

"Shut up, Mallone," said Jessica dismissively.

But Elizabeth detected a quiver of fear in Jessica's voice. Elizabeth was certain they were all thinking the same thing. *What if Heather's right? Maybe the convicts crept up on us while we slept, just moments ago! That means they're still close by. . . .*

Jessica opened her eyes to bright sunlight, feeling groggy and unrested. She stretched out her legs and wiggled her toes, absentmindedly feeling for the sack of gold she'd placed there when she went to sleep. Then, in a flash, she remembered waking up in the middle of the night. *It wasn't a nightmare! My gold is really gone.* She felt the hair on the back of her neck stand on end when she thought of some dirty, scruffy criminals digging around in her sleeping bag.

But when she tried to imagine how the convicts sneaked up on them, it didn't make sense. *We would have noticed if somebody had been following us,* she figured. *It* had *to be Heather.* Then she remembered Heather's lame alibi—that she had been off with Ken. *Not only did she steal my gold, she stole my boyfriend!* Way past groggy now, Jessica was alert and steaming mad. It was time to get to the bottom of this. Where had Heather hidden her gold? She scrambled out of her sleeping bag.

"Time to get moving, you lazyheads," she announced in a loud voice. Bruce moaned next to her.

"Jessica, must you be so predictably obnoxious?" sneered Heather from under her blankets.

"Me, obnoxious? If anyone here's obnoxious, it's you," Jessica countered.

Heather sat straight up, fully awake. "Jessica Wakefield, I am sick and tired of putting up with your asinine ramblings. Why anybody sees you as anything different from the selfish, stuck-up, shallow dumb blonde you are, is quite beyond me."

"Who are you calling a dumb blonde?" Jessica put her hands on her hips and stomped her right foot. "Who's the bimbo who's been whimpering and wailing about escaped prisoners?" she said, her eyes flashing.

"Are you forgetting that I nearly died yesterday? I lost all my stuff—and my gold—and it was your fault!" Heather stood, facing Jessica squarely.

"Who do you think you are, Heather Mallone? You give new meaning to the term 'gold digger'!" Jessica raged. "Don't think for a minute that you'll get away with this. Where did you hide my treasure?"

Elizabeth had never seen her sister so out of control with fury. It was almost scary. And it seemed that no one else in the group was willing to confront the overwhelming hatred that oozed from the two angry girls.

"Are you still harping on that? I told you last night, I don't have your gold, Jessica."

170

"I didn't believe you last night, and I don't believe you now. You have just the devious personality to do something like this."

"Can we talk about devious personality?" screamed Heather. "You're the sneak who tricked us into going after the last treasure when we were supposed to be heading for Desert Oasis. Speaking of devious, I bet you're lying about getting robbed," Heather announced with authority. "You know that you should give your gold to me, and you're squirreling it away somewhere!"

"That's such a lie! You had the motive, you had the opportunity—"

"Nice try, but you forgot one thing . . . I didn't have the opportunity. I have an airtight alibi, right, Ken?" Heather walked over to Ken and hooked her arm through his. He stood without moving.

"I don't want to get involved," he said flatly.

Jessica and Heather looked at him for a moment in silence.

"Don't want to *get involved*?" Heather asked, dropping his arm as if it were hot. "How can you say that?"

"I'm not going to take sides here," Ken repeated.

Hmmm, Ken's not running to Heather's defense, Jessica realized. If she weren't still so angry with him, she might be grateful.

"Ken, after all I've been through, you could be a little nicer," sulked Heather.

"Give it a rest, Heather," Bruce said.

Looking at Ken shuffle his feet, Heather puffed

171

out her lower lip and jammed her hands into her pockets. "I didn't know I was causing you such misery, Ken Matthews," she said sarcastically. "If you didn't want me around anymore, you could have said something."

Heather spun around and marched up the river. Jessica noticed with satisfaction that nobody followed her—not Ken, not even her do-good sister, Elizabeth.

Ken watched Heather flounce up the trail until she disappeared behind a large boulder. He thought back to the night before with a stab of guilt. Seeing Heather and Jessica go at it now, Ken remembered all the things he'd heard Jessica say Heather had done. *I don't like Heather,* he realized. *What was I thinking about last night?*

Nothing much had happened—they had just kissed a couple of times and talked. But with tensions so high between the six of them, the last thing he should do was make things more complicated. Even though his relationship with Jessica had been pretty rocky for the past few days, that was no reason to go and get involved with the girl Jessica hated most in the world. It wasn't right, and Ken knew it. Besides, he felt confident that he and Jessica would patch up their relationship. Just as soon as the trip was over. *Sorry, Heather, you're on your own—buddy system or no buddy system.*

Ken looked over at Jessica. She was standing on top of her sleeping bag, brushing her hair in hard, fast strokes. She wasn't smiling. *Maybe now's not the time to start patching,* Ken thought wryly.

He started rolling up his sleeping bag, sinking onto it when it was tied. No one spoke as they packed their things. *Another high-anxiety moment,* Ken observed. Why didn't any of them have anything to say to each other?

Bruce was muttering to himself as he tossed his sweatshirt and sleep gear into his backpack. Jessica had finished brushing her hair and was now filing her nails with fierce determination. Elizabeth was on her way to the water, doing everything in her power to avoid looking at Todd, who was likewise refusing to look at her.

"Hmmmmm . . . I'll bet I know where Heather's run off to," mused Jessica, breaking the silence. "I'll bet you right now she's digging up *my* gold from where she hid it last night."

"But she was off with your boyfriend last night," Bruce reminded her.

"Oh, shut up, Bruce," Jessica shot back. Bruce's face turned dark. "Do you think I care about that?" she asked, staring at Ken. "I just want my gold back, and I know Heather has it. If it wasn't Heather, it was one of you," she said, looking at everyone, including Elizabeth.

"Jessica, I can't believe you think I'd be capable of stealing anything, much less my own sister's gold," Elizabeth said huffily.

Jessica turned her gaze to Bruce, and Ken noticed the cold stare she gave him. *I guess I don't have to worry about Jess flirting with Bruce anymore,* he concluded.

"Don't look at me. I was out cold until you started screaming your head off," Bruce said defensively. "Why don't you ask Ken if he thinks his buddy stole your gold?" he said with a smirk.

"Uhhh, I don't know," Ken said. Jessica turned and looked at him with accusing eyes. "I mean, I don't think she could have, Jess. I'm sorry, but she was with me. Uh, we were just talking," Ken blurted out.

He could see that although she said she didn't care, she was hurt. Jessica never liked to let others see when she was upset, but Ken could tell that behind her anger and cavalier attitude, it hurt Jessica to think that he had gotten involved with Heather.

"Do you guys think it could have been the convicts?" Todd asked tentatively.

"Oh, please, not you, too, Todd." Jessica rolled her eyes.

"I'm not saying I definitely think it was them, but suppose it was?"

"It's silly to even think about it," Jessica replied.

But Ken wasn't so sure he agreed with her. He *knew* it couldn't have been Heather. That left Bruce, Todd, and Elizabeth. Bruce was the only one Ken could possibly imagine stealing Jessica's gold, but even that seemed unlikely. Bruce was too much of a snob to stoop low enough to steal someone else's treasure.

"This might be a good time to wash out a couple things," Elizabeth commented, breaking Ken's train of thought. "The sun will dry them in no time."

"Are you kidding me?" scoffed Bruce, collecting his stash of water bottles. "I think I'll wait till I get home and let Maria wash them good and proper."

"Besides, this is our last day," Todd said. "What do we need another change of clothes for?" He screwed the top onto the last of his water bottles and walked over to his pack.

Ken glanced up and caught Elizabeth's eye. Seeing the anxious look on her face, Ken could tell Todd's words had struck Elizabeth the same way they'd struck him. *What if this isn't our last day? What if we don't make it back to Desert Oasis in time to meet the bus tonight?*

"Well, Heather's not back yet—might as well get rid of some of the grime we've accumulated," said Jessica, breaking the silence.

"Yeah, good idea," Ken said. The three of them filled the last of their water bottles and went to retrieve their laundry.

Heather picked up a small rock that lay in her path and threw it into the river, watching it toss and spin in the churning rapids until, with a crack, it smashed into a large rock. *I wish that were Jessica's face,* she thought maliciously. She stormed up the riverbank, kicking up dust. *First I almost drown, then I lose all my stuff. And now I'm losing my grip on Ken.*

She wasn't feeling sorry for herself—Heather loathed self-pity. She was angry. *This is not the way my life should be going. Heather Mallone always lands on her feet.*

It was time to plot revenge. "Too bad someone else got to Jessica's gold before I did," she said to herself. Hearing her own words, she stopped cold. No matter what they said, she *knew* the convicts had taken Jessica's gold. She'd had premonitions about meeting up with the convicts ever since she'd heard about their escape.

Feeling droplets of perspiration form on her forehead, Heather realized she'd been walking for quite a while. She paused and turned around to look back the way she'd come. All she saw was the mad, boiling river and the vertical red walls that lined it. No sign of human life. She felt very alone. Camp was far away. *What if they leave without me?* she thought in an uncharacteristic moment of insecurity.

Even those jerks would never be that cruel, she told herself. *Still, I might as well turn back.* She'd just have to figure out some way to return to the scene of her earlier humiliation without losing face.

Just as she was about to turn around and walk back down the riverbank, a strange sound bounced over the roar of the raging water. It sounded like laughter, a man's laughter. Heather didn't breathe, listening to see if the sound came again. It did! And it was definitely male laughter. *Maybe it's just another group out camping,* she told herself, trying to push away the suspicion that was creeping into her consciousness—the suspicion that three armed criminals sat just around the next bend in the river.

Heather couldn't decide what to do. Should she

investigate further? Or should she run for her life? Taking a deep breath, her nose caught the unmistakable odor of cigarettes. *I've got to find out who's out here,* she decided. If it wasn't the convicts, she could put her mind at rest. And if it *was* them, she should warn the others.

Making sure not to crunch any gravel as she walked, Heather crept up to a big boulder and crouched behind it. Peeking her head around the side, her throat tightened with shock. On the other side of the boulder, so close she could almost reach out and touch them, sat three pairs of black work boots! She pulled her head back and panted with fright. As the faint smell of foot odor wafted to her nostrils, Heather wrinkled her nose and shivered. *What do I do now?*

With a slow, effortful breath, Heather placed her now-sweaty palms on the dusty boulder and arched her neck as far as she could. She cocked her head so that her ear faced the men and listened with all her might. Wisps of their conversation threaded through the noise of the river.

"So how much more gold you think they got?" said a gruff voice.

"Lots more—that last mine shaft we checked didn't have nothin'. I know Bert said there was definitely gold in there. I bet those rotten kids just took it all," said another, gruffer voice.

Heather inched closer so that she could get a better look. Two men wearing blue jumpsuits, with their pants rolled up, were lounging by the edge of the river, cooling their feet in the shallow water. Another man sat by himself, whittling a stick with a large hunting knife. And there, sitting by the dead embers of a campfire, was a little plastic Ziploc bag, sparkling in the sunlight. Heather squinted and focused her eyes. There was no doubt about it. Right there, nestled between a canteen and a brown leather jacket, sat Jessica's bag of gold nuggets!

Chapter 12

Jessica fingered the collar of one of her T-shirts, which was spread out on top of her sleeping bag. Amazingly, it was already dry. She folded up the shirt and shorts she'd washed and packed them away in her clean-clothes compartment.

She surveyed the camp. Ken and Elizabeth were folding their clean laundry into their packs, and Todd and Bruce were examining the map. Heather's stuff was still strewn about where she'd left it.

"Looks like we're ready to hit it," announced Jessica, zipping her backpack shut. She knew chances were slim that the rest of the group would just leave Heather, but it was worth a shot.

"Except that Heather hasn't shown up yet," said Ken, looking guilty. "I guess it would be smart to pack up her stuff so that we can get moving as soon as she gets back." But he didn't move. No one did.

Jessica looked over to Elizabeth, expecting her to

jump right in and pack Heather's things. But she was actively preoccupied with flossing her teeth. *Yay— everyone hates Heather!* Jessica thought with glee.

After a heavy silence Todd threw up his hands and started to roll up her sleeping bag. *Looks like my dear sister is losing her reign as the world's biggest do-gooder,* Jessica thought, thoroughly enjoying the moment.

Suddenly Heather burst in on the scene, out of breath and excited.

"You guys! The convicts—the convicts—I saw them!" she blurted between pants. She threw her right arm out, pointing it in the direction from which she'd just come. "I almost walked right into them. It was horrible. I told you they'd find us!" She rested her hand on her chest, which was rising and falling with each gasp of air.

"You can't be serious. Do you actually expect us to believe that crock?" snorted Jessica.

"Wait, Jess," Ken said. "Heather, you're sure you saw them?"

"Oh, Ken, would you stop being so gullible? She's just saying that to try to get your attention. Sorry, Heather, Ken's onto your ploy," said Jessica, facing Heather.

Heather stood her ground. "I'm serious. I heard them talking. They were saying—"

"So now you're hearing voices, are you?" Jessica laughed. "What next, are you going to tell us you were Queen of Sheba in a past life, and therefore we'll need to turn all of our gold over to you—and then carry you on our backs through the desert?"

180

"Would you shut up for a minute so I can tell you?" Heather asked with an exasperated sigh. "I was just walking up the river, minding my own business, when I heard this laughter. So I hid behind a boulder and saw these three men wearing blue jumpsuits, smoking cigarettes. They were talking about us! They know we have gold. And I saw your gold, Jessica. They had it in a plastic bag!"

"Oh, right. There you go trying to make me believe you didn't steal it yourself. Pitiful, Heather, just pitiful. You're never going to pull one over on me with that lame story. I know you went off to retrieve my gold from where you hid it last night," Jessica accused. "Someone hold her down while I search her!" She moved toward Heather, but Ken stepped in and blocked her way.

He put his hand up, gesturing for Jessica to stop, and said in a calm voice, "I'm not saying I believe Heather—about the convicts. But I know she didn't take your gold, Jess." Jessica narrowed her eyes and peered at Ken through the slits. He put his hand gently on her arm, leading her away from the group.

Once out of earshot, he spoke to her in a low voice. "Let's say she does have your gold, for argument's sake. You don't want to stoop to her level, Jess—there's no way she'll get away with it. Let's wait for her to come clean."

Jessica looked into Ken's face. He seemed totally sincere. He was back on her side! She almost threw her arms around him in a big hug, until she remembered how he'd betrayed her. She frowned.

181

It's going to take a lot more than that to get me to like you again, she thought.

"I'm sorry, Jess, about everything," Ken whispered, understanding Jessica's silent statement. "I'd like to make it up to you, if you'll let me." He gazed at her with longing. He looked so adorable standing there, pushing his hair off his face in that cute way that he did, it was all Jessica could do not to grant him forgiveness right there on the spot.

"Doesn't anyone believe me?" screeched Heather, interrupting Jessica's moment of weakness. "You've got to. Why would I make this up?"

"Because you're trying to hide the fact that you're a thief!" pronounced Jessica, turning away from Ken.

"I'm not. I swear. Listen, we're in danger." Jessica watched with satisfaction as everyone stared at the ground.

"Ever hear the story about the boy who cried 'wolf'?" Bruce asked with a grin.

"Yeah, Heather, you have been awfully fixated on those convicts. Remember how you kept thinking you saw them on the trail, and it just turned out to be a boulder?" Ken said.

"That was just me being nervous. Now I'm totally serious." But no one was buying it. They'd heard her express her paranoia about the convicts too often. Jessica was elated.

Heather threw up her hands in defeat. "Well, even though you don't believe me, *I* know there are three dangerous criminals breathing down our necks. We'd better get moving." She started to

182

collect her things, and Todd bent to finish rolling up her now-dry sleeping bag.

Jessica raised her eyebrows as she saw Heather give Todd a winsome look. *She struck out with my boyfriend, so now she's moving in on my sister's!* Although she wouldn't wish Heather on anybody, Jessica had to admit that she was not altogether unhappy with this turn of events. *The way she's been acting so high-and-mighty on this trip, Elizabeth deserves to have the rug pulled out from under her,* Jessica thought vindictively.

Shading her eyes from the high sun, Elizabeth looked toward the horizon. Heat waves distorted the distant mountains, making them bounce and wiggle. Trying to focus, she realized it wasn't just the heat waves that were affecting her vision; she was dizzy. She needed water.

Elizabeth unclipped her canteen from her belt and threw back her head, gulping down what must have been a whole pint of water. Running her tongue along the inside of her mouth, she thought of Kay's warnings about bacteria. *Well, if this water does have bacteria, I certainly wouldn't be able to feel it with my tongue,* she chided herself.

She took one last swig, noticing that her canteen was dangerously light. *Have I drunk this much already?*

"How much longer till we get there?" she called out to Bruce. He was loping along at a brisk pace, almost out of earshot.

"We should make it to the last treasure by early

afternoon," Bruce barked back without slowing down. Since Ken hadn't volunteered for navigation duties, and Elizabeth wanted no part of this detour, Bruce had assumed the responsibility. Elizabeth knew he'd done a good deal of sailing, so she figured he must have some idea of what he was doing.

Elizabeth saw Bruce scramble up the sheer face of a large boulder and disappear over its top. She paused at the bottom and looked up. It was nearly fifteen feet high, and she didn't see any footholds. Bruce was long gone. *What happened to the buddy system? How am I going to get up there without a helping hand?* she asked herself.

Resigned, Elizabeth pressed up against the boulder, remembering the rock-climbing techniques she'd learned in training. *Sometimes you can feel what you can't see,* she reminded herself. She shut her eyes and raised her arms above her head, skimming the rock's face until her left hand found a small ridge to grip, then her right. *Hand, feet, hand, feet,* she said to herself over and over, as she made her way up the boulder.

Then her right hand fell flat. She'd made it to the top—all by herself! With one last push Elizabeth scurried onto the boulder and stood up. She looked back and saw four haggard figures silently trudging single file up the trail, approaching the base of the boulder. *If I can make it, they can, too,* she thought, swiveling on her heels.

But as she marched onward, she realized with a sinking feeling that even she had lost the spirit of cooperation, of teamwork. It was more than the buddy system that had broken down. *It's every man for himself—I mean woman.*

Jessica watched Todd's feet disappear over the boulder.

"Can I get some help here?" she called up to him. His face popped back over the ledge. With the deep-blue sky framing his face, it looked to Jessica as if Todd's head were floating, unattached to a body.

"You're just going to have to feel your way up, Jess. There's not much I can do for you," he said, sounding unconcerned. Then he was gone.

"But—" Jessica looked around. She was the last of the group to reach the boulder. She was all on her own. *Well, seeing as both Elizabeth and Heather could do this, I sure can,* Jessica told herself, revving up her courage.

That wasn't so bad, she realized when she'd made it to the top. Brushing the dust off her hands and the front of her shirt, she turned to continue the hike. Todd and the rest of the group looked like tiny dolls in the distance. *It must have taken longer than I realized to climb that wall.*

She hurried after them. Walking with long, powerful strides, Jessica felt her hips creak and ache with the effort, noticing that the pain made her aware of other areas that ached—her lower back, her calves, her right pinkie toe rubbing against the hard leather of her boot. *What I wouldn't do for a leisurely bubble bath right about now,* she thought longingly. *A cool one.*

But she had to maintain her concentration. The day was moving at a brisk pace, and they still had quite a way to go to get to the treasure. Then they had to make it to Desert Oasis by seven o'clock. Jessica felt a slow wave of guilt spread over her for leading the group astray. *Maybe Elizabeth was right. Maybe I shouldn't have led us in search of more treasure.*

But if there was one emotion she hated, it was guilt. *It didn't look that far on the map. I couldn't have known it was this much out of the way,* she justified to herself. And with Heather's gold on the bottom of the river, they *had* to find more. Once they got to the next treasure, everyone would be thanking her for increasing their stockpile. Everything would be fine, just as soon as she got Heather to cough up the gold she had stolen.

Hurrying to catch up with the others, Jessica noticed that they'd stopped up ahead. When she reached them, she saw why. There, plopped right in their path, sprawled a huge boulder field.

"We should stop for lunch now before we attempt to cross this," Elizabeth said.

Jessica rolled her eyes. *There she goes again, telling everyone what to do.*

"C'mon, Liz. Let's just get across this boulder field, then we'll stop," Todd countered.

"Remember what Brad said about getting over boulders? The most important thing is maintaining good balance. If we're light-headed from hunger, it's that much more dangerous," Elizabeth maintained.

Jessica had to admit that Elizabeth had a point.

But she wasn't about to side with her sister the know-it-all.

"I still say we should go and not lose momentum," Todd argued. "What does everyone else think?"

"Let's get it over with," Ken said. Jessica saw the others nod in agreement, so she did, too.

"OK, if you guys really feel strong enough. Be careful, everyone," cautioned Elizabeth.

"Yes, Mother," Jessica mocked. Elizabeth threw her a nasty look before taking a swig of water. Jessica just smiled broadly until she felt her lower lip crack. *Ouch.* She dug some lip balm out of her pack.

"Hey, Jess, can I have some of that?" Ken asked. Jessica noticed Heather fumble for her own lip balm, but she wasn't quick enough.

"Sure," said Jessica, cheerfully placing the tube in his outstretched hand.

"Ahh, that feels good," he said after he'd rubbed some on. Heather scowled.

Ken announced he was going up. "The boulders all seem to be about four feet apart," he described after he'd climbed to the top. "Climbing up and down, up and down, is out of the question. The best way to cross this field is to leap from one boulder to the next." He bent into a crouch and hurled his body to the next boulder, landing smoothly.

"It's not too bad!" he called back to the waiting group.

"Ken! Buddy! Wait up!" Heather shouted.

"C'mon up, Heather," Ken urged without slowing down.

Jessica's face broke into a huge grin as she watched

Heather scurry up the rock, fruitlessly trying to catch up with Ken. *At least that's one thing I don't have to worry about anymore,* she told herself.

Meanwhile, Ken had forged ahead out of sight; Jessica could gauge his progress only by the sound of his grunts and the clap of his boots landing on rock. One by one, they all climbed to the top of the first boulder and started leaping.

This is almost fun—kind of like a cheerleading grand finale, Jessica thought as she tightened her thigh muscles for another leap. *And a perfect landing, if I do say so myself.* She crossed the boulder and aimed her body for the next.

"Ken! Check out my Y-leap!" Heather called out. It seemed Heather had the same thought as Jessica. She was embellishing her leaps, carelessly throwing her body into kicks, splits, and twists.

"If you break your ankle, Heather, we're not carrying you out of here," Jessica warned.

"Yeah, Heather, cut it out," Todd said as Heather mounted a full triple herky.

She's never going to be able to land this, Jessica realized, with visions of Heather's skull cracked open on the rocks. She watched with horror as Heather seemed to lose her center of gravity. Heather realized her error in midair and let out a frightened squeal. A split second later she crumpled onto the next boulder with a scream.

"Heather!" everyone shouted in unison. "Are you OK?"

"My ankle! My ankle!" Heather wailed, grabbing her leg. "I think I've sprained it!"

Chapter 13

"Gentle, gentle, it hurts!" Heather sobbed as Todd wound an Ace bandage around her ankle.

"I'm being as gentle as I can, Heather. You'll be OK, just hold still," Todd soothed, cradling her leg in his arms. Heather sniffled loudly.

Elizabeth turned her attention to her own aching feet, trying to stifle her feelings of jealousy. *He's just being nice to try to calm her down,* she told herself, tying and retying her bootlaces.

Ken handed Todd a small bottle of disinfectant from his first-aid kit.

"Now this is going to hurt a little," Todd said softly. "You skinned your knee pretty badly." Heather yelped as Todd rubbed the disinfectant onto the wound. Elizabeth noticed that Todd's hand strayed momentarily to Heather's smooth, tanned calf.

"At least you don't have your pack to carry,"

Ken said ironically. Elizabeth noticed the warmth in his voice; his earlier coldness toward Heather seemed to have melted with this latest catastrophe. Elizabeth bristled. *What do these guys see in her?*

"I'll say," agreed Todd. "Luckily, we've almost reached the last boulder. I'll help Heather climb down off of here—I'm sure we can squeeze a trail through to the end."

"Don't let me fall," cried Heather, reaching out for Todd's outstretched arms.

"I won't, Heather," he said reassuringly. Elizabeth, Bruce, Ken, and Jessica watched the two slowly make their way down the dusty boulder.

"Made it!" Todd called up to their waiting faces. "Go on and continue hurdling over—we'll meet you on the other side!"

"Careful, you two," called Ken. "Take your time."

As Elizabeth put her pack back on, she felt a huge wave of vexation spread from her head to her toes. It was so powerful, she almost felt dizzy. *If Heather had been wearing boots like she was supposed to, this never would have happened,* she thought angrily. She leaped to the next boulder, landing with an emphatic grunt.

Finally she landed atop the last boulder and scrambled down.

"Well, we might as well eat lunch while we wait for Todd and Heather to make their way through. There's some shade under that outcrop," Ken said, pointing to a shelter a few feet away.

Under the shadow of an overhang Bruce threw off his pack with disgust. "Of all Heather's stupid stunts, this has got to be the worst."

"Tell me about it," Jessica muttered, slumping on top of her pack.

"Oh, don't let me get started on you, Wakefield. You're about as bad a ditz as Mallone," Bruce said. Jessica tightened her mouth and slanted her eyes into her most venomous expression.

But before she could zing Bruce with a comeback, Heather and Todd appeared between two boulders. With Heather's arms wrapped tightly around Todd's broad shoulders, he was basically carrying her on his back.

"Oh, Todd, what would I have done without you!" Heather gushed, burying her face in Todd's neck.

Elizabeth was well past her boiling point. "Doesn't she just make you sick?" she spat under her breath to Jessica. Jessica looked at Elizabeth blankly and didn't respond. Elizabeth knew her sister was mad at her, but she thought Jessica's hatred toward Heather would neutralize any other feelings. She was right.

"I hate Heather Mallone more than I've ever hated anyone in the world," grumbled Jessica after a moment.

Elizabeth smiled to herself—she knew Jessica was glad to have an ally against her nemesis. *Maybe I should get over my anger with Jess so I can stop feeling so absolutely alone,* she thought.

After Todd helped Heather sit down, they all

191

started eating lunch. Elizabeth really wasn't hungry, but she forced herself to take bite after bite.

Packing her lunch wrapper in her pack, Elizabeth looked up at the sky. Clouds had appeared seemingly out of nowhere, spotting the sky, which had been clear and dazzling bright just hours ago. She watched clouds of dust swirl as the wind picked up.

According to Bruce, they were supposed to head up a steep, dusty embankment. *If the rain comes now, this will be mud.* Elizabeth pictured all of them sliding and rolling haphazardly down to the bottom of the valley, crushed against boulders. They'd be buried under mounds of mud. *We're so off course by now that no one even knows where we are. How could they find us?*

"We'd better get moving. Those clouds look ominous," Bruce observed starkly.

Even Bruce was getting worried, Elizabeth realized with dismay. She could have used a little of his nonchalant attitude right about now.

Todd pulled Heather up to her feet, but when she tried to put weight on her bad ankle, her leg gave out.

"It really hurts!" she complained. She hobbled along, leaning on Todd. Their progress was slow. One by one, more clouds dotted the sky. Elizabeth felt panic rise from deep within her. *Now, with one of our party injured, we'll never make it back to Desert Oasis before this storm hits!*

"I'm sorry, Heather, I've reached my limit," Todd said, stopping to rub his shoulders. "Somebody else has to help Heather for a while."

The group came to a halt. Heather stood on one foot, looking straight at Ken.

"I'll give you a hand," Ken obliged, looking resigned.

"Thanks," Heather cooed as Ken circled his arms around her waist. Elizabeth saw Jessica glare at them icily.

The hill was relentless. Tiny pebbles rained down under Elizabeth's feet, and twice she almost lost her footing. Through the sprinkling of clouds, the sun still burned fiercely on her back.

"Jess? Liz? Do you think the both of you could support Heather between you?" Ken called after what seemed like an hour of hiking.

Elizabeth met Jessica's eye. She knew what her twin was thinking—no way! But Elizabeth realized that keeping Heather moving was the only chance they had to reach safety. *Looks like we've got to cooperate,* she told herself.

But she didn't want Jessica to think she'd lost an ally. "We could probably do it," Elizabeth said with an exaggerated sigh, gazing at Jessica with compassion. She hoped her twin could read the reluctance in her eyes. Jessica was obstinate.

"I'm not about to help that brat," Jessica said haughtily.

"Well, excuse me!" huffed Heather.

"C'mon, Jess, we've got to pull together now," said Ken wearily.

"I said no." Jessica crossed her arms in front of her. "Do you really think she's as hurt as she says? After all her ankle twisting, blisters, and other ailments? Give me a break. You don't see Elizabeth or me begging for help."

"She's really hurt, Jess," Todd said. He turned to Elizabeth. "Liz? Do you think you could talk some sense into your sister?"

But Jessica's words had a ring of truth to Elizabeth. Heather had suffered one calamity after another, and Elizabeth was sick of it. "I'm not my sister's keeper, Todd," Elizabeth replied brusquely.

"Jeez! I'll take her up the hill," said Bruce suddenly. "I swear—if we weren't so close to the treasure, I'd be outta here."

"I thought you said we'd reach the treasure in the early afternoon," whined Heather.

"Stop complaining, Mallone," Bruce retorted. "Just be glad we didn't leave you on the side of the trail."

The sun was getting lower and lower in the sky. A group of black ravens squawked and circled overhead. Jessica's heart sank to her toes as she admitted to herself that they were never going to make the rendezvous with the bus.

When they finally reached the top of the butte, the sun was rapidly disappearing behind the horizon. Although the colors of the sunset

194

were brilliant, Jessica could think only of the black night that faced them.

"Over this way," directed Bruce, leading them onto a narrow trail with orange walls rising on either side. "The cave with the treasure should be along here somewhere.

"I think we're getting close," Bruce said after they'd been winding around for a bit. "Here, this must be it!" he hollered, coming upon a dark crack in the wall of rock.

Without saying a word, they all dropped their packs and fished out their flashlights—by now the routine was familiar. But as she entered the darkness of the cave, Jessica shuddered with apprehension. *This doesn't feel good.*

They crept through the darkness, Bruce in the lead. Rounding a corner, Bruce suddenly stopped short, grabbing the rock to his side and gasping for air.

"What is it?" Elizabeth peered over Bruce's shoulder. "Ohmigosh!" she screamed.

Jessica and the rest gathered behind Elizabeth to see what was going on. Jessica blinked, then blinked again. She'd had enough biology to recognize the sight. Skeletons! Human skeletons!

Jessica heard shrill screams bouncing off the cave walls. After a moment she realized they were coming from her own throat. She couldn't breathe, but her body reacted automatically. She stumbled backward against the cave wall. In the dark silence Jessica heard the others whimper and pant.

Finally Bruce moved. He pointed his flashlight

and walked toward the pile of bones. "I count six," he said, nudging a skull with his boot.

"Bruce! Don't!" cried Jessica.

"What's the matter, Wakefield? Scared of some old bones? They're dead now." But even in the dim light Jessica could see that the blood had drained from his face.

"Looks like there's another satchel over there." Bruce walked around the skeletons and picked up a leather bag lying against a rock. He loosened the buckle and peered inside. "Yaaaaa!" he screamed suddenly, dropping the satchel as if it had burned his hands. The flap fell open, and Jessica watched in horror as a swarm of scorpions oozed out.

"I just know those skeletons must be the people who we read about in the diary," Elizabeth said, thinking out loud more than she was talking to anyone. She had wanted to see if there was a diary somewhere among the bones. But the scorpions, free from their confinement, had spread quickly over the ground, forcing them to make a quick retreat out of the cave.

"That's so creepy," Todd murmured with a shiver.

"Isn't it? I mean, they almost seemed like us—" Elizabeth stopped herself midsentence. But she knew they'd all made the connection. *Six of them, six of us.* Greed had infiltrated those explorers, just as it had them. *Have we just come face-to-face with our fate?*

They made their way back to the ledge of the butte and looked out over the desert bowl. The air crackled with dry heat. The clouds Elizabeth saw appear earlier in the day had multiplied and merged, looking heavy and foreboding, with glints of lightning flashing in their depths. The sound of thunder bellowed in the distance.

"It's seven o'clock," Todd said quietly. Elizabeth pictured the bus waiting for them at Desert Oasis, miles away. Kay and Brad were probably sitting in the front seat, casually waiting for their young charges to appear. What would they think when there was no sign of the group?

They had only enough food for tonight's dinner. And with their pace slowed by Heather's injury, it would be a while before they could brave the mud and floods the storm was sure to cause. Not to mention the convicts. Elizabeth had no doubt about it anymore. After everything that had happened, she believed Heather. Somewhere out there three dangerous criminals were probably winding their way through the desert in pursuit of their gold. *I can't believe we've ended up like this,* she thought despairingly.

"Are you happy now, Jessica? See where your scheming has gotten us?" Elizabeth no longer wanted to make amends with her sister—she would never forgive Jessica for putting their lives in mortal danger.

Jessica opened her mouth to respond, but

Elizabeth could see that she had nothing to say in her own defense.

"No, let's hear it, Jessica. I'd love to know how you're going to weasel your way out of this one," Heather snarled when Jessica didn't speak.

"We could have made it just fine if you weren't such a weak, helpless sap!" snapped Jessica.

"Shut up! Just shut up! How can you even say such a thing when we all know this is all your fault!" Todd interrupted with uncharacteristic venom.

"We can sit here and lay blame, or we can figure out what to do!" Ken shouted over everyone's bickering. And he was right. They had to focus on a solution.

But before Elizabeth could organize her thoughts to form a plan, her attention was jolted to the drama above. The storm clouds had moved with quickening speed; they were directly overhead. Lightning streaked like gunfire through the clouds, and volleys of thunder shook the air. The wind rose. A bolt of lightning flickered over the butte, setting a nearby sagebrush immediately ablaze. Someone screamed.

Then the water came down. It didn't fall, it attacked—huge pellets of rain plastered Elizabeth's shirt to her back. And driving wind blew stinging water into her eyes, blinding her. The only sound she could make out was the roar of thunder.

She cowered against a wall of rock to take advantage of the scant protection it provided. *We're doomed.*

The Sweet Valley gang is facing hunger, thirst, flash floods . . . and three escaped convicts. Find out if Jessica and Elizabeth can survive the ultimate desert challenge, in Sweet Valley High #116, **Nightmare in Death Valley.**

Bantam Books in the Sweet Valley High series
Ask your bookseller for the books you have missed

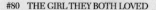
=have

SIGN UP FOR THE SWEET VALLEY HIGH® FAN CLUB!

Hey, girls! Get all the gossip on Sweet Valley High's® most popular teenagers when you join our fantastic Fan Club! As a member, you'll get all of this really cool stuff:

- Membership Card with your own personal Fan Club ID number
- A Sweet Valley High® Secret Treasure Box
- Sweet Valley High® Stationery
- Official Fan Club Pencil (for secret note writing!)
- Three Bookmarks
- A "Members Only" Door Hanger
- Two Skeins of J. & P. Coats® Embroidery Floss with flower barrette instruction leaflet
- Two editions of *The Oracle* newsletter
- Plus exclusive Sweet Valley High® product offers, special savings, contests, and much more!

Be the first to find out what Jessica & Elizabeth Wakefield are up to by joining the Sweet Valley High® Fan Club for the one-year membership fee of only $6.25 each for U.S. residents, $8.25 for Canadian residents (U.S. currency). Includes shipping & handling.

Send a check or money order (do not send cash) made payable to "Sweet Valley High® Fan Club" along with this form to:

SWEET VALLEY HIGH® FAN CLUB, BOX 3919-B, SCHAUMBURG, IL 60168-3919

NAME _____
(Please print clearly)

ADDRESS _____

CITY_____ STATE _____ ZIP_____
(Required)

AGE _____ BIRTHDAY _____ / _____ / _____

Offer good while supplies last. Allow 6-8 weeks after check clearance for delivery. Addresses without ZIP codes cannot be honored. Offer good in USA & Canada only. Void where prohibited by law.
©1993 by Francine Pascal   LCI-1383-123